Last To

TO ARTHUR + BABS

BEST WISHES

DAVE

Last Tango in Liverpool

David Tollerton

liverpool books online

www.lasttangoinliverpool.co.uk

Last Tango in Liverpool

First Published in 2002 liverpool books online
www.lasttangoinliverpool.co.uk
Copyright © David Tollerton 2002

The right of David Tollerton to be identified as
the author of this work has been asserted in
accordance with sections 77 and 78 of the
Copyright Designs and Patents Act 1988.

Printed in Great Britain by Biddles Ltd
www.biddles.co.uk

With thanks to
Andrea for being sensible
Bob for his encouragement
Linda for being 100% proof
and J.K. for his expertise

Last Tango in Liverpool

Book One

1

Knotty Ash, Liverpool
January 1959
Saturday
4-30pm

Billy Walsh tied up the laces of his patent leather shoes and whistled Hernando's Hideaway, a popular song from the musical, The Pyjama Game. Billy liked the song It was a tango and Billy loved dancing the tango.

He straightened up and looked in the mirror. His shark-skin suit was crisp and sharp, just back from the dry cleaners. With it he wore a silk shirt and a polka dot tie. He ran his fingers through his hair and the thick black curls fell back into place. He liked what he saw. He was a good-looking man of five-feet ten inches and though a little overweight at fourteen stone, he carried it well. He had a scar under his right eye and one of his front teeth was chipped, a legacy of an irate husband. But this did not subdue his jaunty manner and never deterred Billy from going back for more.

Billy was a Liverpool Yank, a Cunard man, an able-bodied donkeyman on the Liverpool to New York run. He was also a ladies' man, a man who liked to dance, liked to drink and liked to gamble. He was single, earned plenty of money and liked to spend it.

He was envied by most other men, but disliked by some, especially husbands, because he considered most women fair game.

It was January 1959 and the Walsh household were preparing to celebrate the fact that Billy's younger brother Tommy had just been demobbed from the army. As he was in Germany at Christmas, and Billy was in New York, it was decided to delay the festivities until they were both home. Tommy was twenty-five, a couple of inches taller than Billy, fair-haired and lean. With his hair in the crew-cut style of the day,' he looked a little like Jeff Chandler, a film star of the fifties. Unlike Billy, Tommy didn't play around. He had been courting Betty for a couple of years and everyone expected that they would marry sooner or later.

Tommy had been a good soldier for most of the seven years he served in the King's Regiment. In four years he had made sergeant, but after beating up a bullying bar-owner in Nairobi, he was busted to private. It took him two more years to make corporal, and that's how he was demobbed, Corporal Driver Tommy Walsh.

Billy came down stairs. He was just about ready to leave, to collect Ruby, who he met the previous night at the Locarno. He was singing along with Frankie Laine's Jealousy, another tango, playing on his sister's Dansette record player. He brushed his overcoat and placed his white silk scarf carefully around his neck.

'I'm off now,' he announced. 'We'll see you all

in the Knotty Ash Hotel at eight o'clock.' With that the front door closed and he strode down the path.

Kate was quick to her feet. Off came Frankie Laine and on went Cliff Richard singing Livin' Doll.

'Never mind that!' shouted Mrs Walsh. 'Come and help me finish this buffet.'

Kate went into the kitchen to assist her mother. She was looking forward to the night, as she was just eighteen and was to be allowed to join the family in the pub for the first time. Kate was like her mother, small and dark. Her hair was as black as coal and it glistened in the light. Her small nose and a generous mouth gave her a Mediterranean look.

Time had been unkind to Mrs Walsh. She had delivered seven children, but only four had survived. The early years married to Jack had been hard and she looked older than her fifty-two years.

Jack had been a tough man in his day, a well known 'scrapper' and political agitator on the docks. Most people were persuaded to vote with Jack when hands had to be raised. Some said Jack had served time for robbing a post office, though no one really knew the truth and no one wanted to be the first to ask. Jack had injured his back five years ago, loading whisky into a ship's hold and now, at fifty-seven, he was out of work. His blond hair had turned white and a absence of physical exercise had resulted in a quite noticeable

5

paunch. Now, he kept himself to himself, no longer a regular drinker. His pleasure was smoking his Black Shag hand-rolling tobacco while leaning on his front gate.

In Tommy, Mrs Walsh could see the young Jack, though thank God, she thought, he doesn't have his father's temper.

Another record blared out from the record player, You've Got What it Takes, by Marv Johnson. Kate ran into the living room. She was angry. Everyone used her record player without so much as a by-your-leave. This time it was Bobby, the youngest in the family at fifteen.

'Leave my things alone!' Kate screamed. Bobby mimicked her just as his father came into the room.

'That's enough,' he said. 'Turn that thing off and put the radio on for the football results.'

Bobby said, 'In a sec, Dad,'

'Right now!' Jack thundered at him. 'You'll have all night to play records when we're out. Now go and get your bath and let me listen to the football results.'

Bobby trudged off. He was none too pleased at being left behind in the house, though his mate, Dave, from next door was being allowed to keep him company and they would be allowed a couple of bottles of pale ale.

Bobby couldn't wait for summer to come along. He would be leaving school and hoped to follow Billy into the merchant navy. He had blond curly hair and a fresh face full of freckles. A neat and tidy boy. He liked a lot of the early black rock 'n' roll and would pester Billy to bring him records back from New York. Chuck Berry and Little Richard were his favourites.

Mrs Walsh and Kate were putting the finishing touches to the buffet. There were spare ribs, pork pies, sausage rolls, ham, cheese and turkey sandwiches, pickled onions, gherkins, home made mince pies and sherry trifles. She had been saving for months for this night and now it was going to be extra special.

Billy was bringing a young lady home.

2

5 o'clock

Billy walked briskly up the avenue. It was cold but dry. The remnants of snow from earlier in the week lay packed in the gutters and against the privet hedges. Billy stepped carefully. He didn't want his shoes marked and he hoped the weather would get no worse. Having spent the last two hours getting ready, he didn't want his appearance spoiled by the weather.

Skipping across a side road, he made a tango-like lurch as though he was holding Ruby around the waist. Ruby, Ruby. Since he'd woken up mid-morning he had repeated her name constantly.

Reaching the top of the avenue, he crossed the duel carriageway and made for the bus stop. There wouldn't be long to wait as it was a main route into the city and well served by buses. Plenty of time, he thought as he checked his watch: five past five. He had arranged to meet Ruby at six o'clock in the Cygnet Hotel, on the corner of Prescot Road and Derby Lane in Old Swan.

He was the only one at the bus stop. The road was quiet and he lit a cigarette, a Pall Mall. He brought two hundred ashore with him because he liked the toasted flavour. They were one of the things Ruby had noticed about him in the Locarno the night before.

She had asked Billy if she could have a cigarette.

'Sure,' he said. 'If I can have a dance.'

'It's a deal,' she said, and moved towards the dance-floor.

'Not yet.' Billy his hand gently on her arm. 'Have your smoke first and we'll wait for a tango.'

'That suits me,' Ruby said. 'But I hope you can tango. Most men think they can, but they just end up throwing the woman around.'

'Oh, I can tango,' Billy said, as he lit her cigarette. 'Would you like a drink to go with that?'

'Vodka and orange, please,' she replied with a smile.

Billy ordered her drink and added a Highball for himself. He watched her as she enjoyed the Pall Mall and thought she looked more than just a little attractive. She had green eyes, though that might have been a trick of the lighting, and a full figure. At least a thirty-eight inch bust, Billy decided. Maybe a little thick around the waist, but she carried no flab. Her legs were shapely, but what excited him was her hands. They were long and elegant. Her fingernails were well manicured and painted crimson red. She knew he was looking at her and asked for another cigarette.

He obliged.

'Are you on your own?' he asked.

She told him she was with a couple of girlfriends who were on the dance-floor, jiving.

He hesitated to ask if she was married. There

was no ring, but something told him she was.

The jive number finished. A few people left the floor and the band struck up a tango: Sway, a Dean Martin number and just what Billy was waiting for. He took her by the waist and led her on to the dance-floor.

He remembered she felt good as he held her close. She was firm and her perfume was inviting as she pressed herself against him. Billy knew he was going to enjoy this.

She matched him step for step.

Billy held her as close as he dared. He could feel her breast against him. His thigh touched hers as they executed a sharp turn. He let her lie in his right arm.

She arched her back over his right leg and Billy bent over her, their mouths close and her breath coming in sharp gasps as her bosom heaved.

Billy snatched her upright, spun her around and propelled her across the dance-floor.

The other dancers made room for them. Some stopped dancing to watch. Ruby allowed herself to be carried along with the euphoria. She clung to Billy, feeling sensuous and uninhibited. No one had ever danced with her like this before. She never once took her eyes off Billy's face and when the music stopped, their lips brushed before she realised people were watching. Reluctantly, she pulled her head away.

There were gasps and whistles from the crowd as they left the floor.

'Another drink?' Billy said.

'I need one after that,' she answered with an exhilarated smile. 'And a smoke,'

As they reached the bar, Ruby's friends appeared. One of them asked if she was returning to their table, but Ruby indicated she was staying with Billy.

It was just the sign Billy was looking for. He knew he was 'on' now.

The number 10 bus pulled up with a screech of brakes. Don't they ever service these things, thought Billy, as he ground out his cigarette. He skipped on board.

'Single to Derby Lane,' he told the conductor.

'Fourp'nce,' the man replied, as he flicked out a ticket from the machine. 'I see Liverpool could only draw today,' he said

'Oh, yeah,' Billy answered with indifference. Football was not his scene. He climbed the stairs for a seat up top so he could smoke. He lit another cigarette and inhaled deeply.

The bus reached St Oswald Street and Billy prepared to alight. It was only five-thirty and he had half-an-hour to kill, so he went first to the Red House across the road and bought himself a Highball. Billy was not a beer drinker. As far as he was concerned, the only thing you got from beer was a big belly.

Most of the talk in the pub was of Liverpool's late equaliser at Grimsby Town and Everton's comfortable win against Burnley at Goodison Park. Billy took himself to a quiet end of the bar and took in the barmaid. She was friendly and quite attractive, so Billy pulled her leg a little and found out her name was Carol. She finished at eight most nights and her day off was Thursday. She liked going to the cinema and was crazy about Tab Hunter. Billy said he might just be around on Wednesday night and was thinking of going to the cinema himself on Thursday.

'If you fancy it,' he said with a flash of his teeth, 'I'll take you.'

'Ask me again on Wednesday,' she answered with a coy smile. But Billy knew what she was really saying.

'I'll do that.'

He checked his watch: Five fifty-five. 'See you Wednesday,' he said, finishing his drink. Always worth keeping something in reserve, he thought.

Back outside, he crossed the road and made his way to the Cygnet pub.

Billy had taken Ruby home by taxi the previous night. She wouldn't invite him into the house and he had to settle for the piece of waste ground behind the jewellers shop on the corner. This was a disappointment to Billy, but Ruby made up for it. There was no street lighting to inhibit them and Ruby led him into an alcove at the rear entrance to the jewellers. It was cold and Ruby was wearing a long fur coat. She opened it up and Billy put his hands inside. He loosened her waspie belt and unbuttoned her blouse. He could just make out the swell of her breasts above her bra. His temples began to throb as she pulled his head close to her. Her mouth was open, her lips moist and luscious as she kissed him fiercely, her tongue darting around his mouth. Billy pressed his mouth hard against hers, his hands now caressing her breasts. He found her nipple through her bra. She took his hands and guided them round her back to the bra clasp. The bra fell forward and her breasts, large and firm, were exposed. Her nipples were hard and Billy bent his head and deftly took one in his mouth. His teeth gently nipped at it.

Ruby moaned. By this time she had undone his belt and fly and her hand was inside his shorts. Billy was erect and Ruby's elegant, long hands stroked him, her fingernails digging in slightly. It was a pain of pleasure.

He reached inside her skirt and into her panties. She was wet. She opened her legs to allow him to caress her. By now she was close to reaching a climax.

The sheer excitement of the situation caused it to be over all too quickly. Ruby hurriedly covered herself up and said she must go. Billy wanted to see her again. He wanted to do things properly. He wanted her in bed. He told her about the delayed Christmas party and she agreed to meet him the following at six o'clock in the Cygnet.

Billy had just finished his Highball as she entered.

It was ten past six.

3

Piccadilly, London
6 o'clock

Stavros Ziacos was a wealthy man. He owned three Greek restaurants and a large house in Greenfield Vale, just off Prescot Road, with a jewellers shop on the corner. He didn't suffer fools. His staff sweated blood. He was a bully. He was married to a red-haired beauty called Ruby.

Stavros was a jealous man. He was also a wife beater and having now spent two days in London without Ruby meant he was in a foul mood. On the Thursday evening, as he was leaving for London, he had insisted Ruby should go with him. When she refused, he had slapped her across the face, punched her in the stomach and promised her more of the same when he returned. Only the fact that there was an important deal to conclude persuaded him to travel without her. The deal, to be finalised over the weekend, would keep him in London until Monday morning, by which time he would be a partner in a ten restaurant chain in Liverpool, Birmingham and London.

He was five-foot eight inches tall and at sixteen stones, he never looked comfortable. He perspired easily and his clothes always looked too tight for him. No matter that they were hand-made to measure and cost a pretty penny. He was dark shaven, with thick black hair and heavy eyebrows. He liked to wear gold rings and bracelets and a diamond tie stud. He smoked half-coronas, up to twenty a day, and he enjoyed food and red wine in copious amounts.

As a young man in Athens, he was a street trader in trinkets, mostly worthless, but the soldiers were mugs, especially the Americans. After the war, they would buy anything from a fifteen-year-old street urchin. He had to be tough and on one occasion beat a couple of other young traders senseless and secured their territory. Soon, he had a dozen boys selling for him and four more keeping them in line.

He soon moved on to prostitution and in the decade following the war he accumulated a small fortune. He regularly transferred money to English banks and in 1955, aged twenty-six, he was able to buy his first restaurant, in Liverpool. In three years, he had three restaurants, two in Liverpool and one in Birkenhead. He worked hard and bullied his way to success. With his two 'minders' he would check and double check every record and receipt, and the manager who stepped out of line was ruthlessly dealt with. Nobody took advantage of Stavros.

When opening his third restaurant in Birkenhead in the spring of 1958, he met Ruby. She and her friends were there on the opening night. Stavros was besotted, He wanted her and didn't care who knew it. He sent wine to the table.

'On the house,' the waiter said, 'paid for by the owner, Mr Ziacos.' After the meal, he sent liqueurs. 'On the house again,' said the waiter, with a wink.

Stavros insisted that Alex, his chauffeur, run Ruby and her friends home.

'But we live in Liverpool,' Ruby said.

'No problem,' said Stavros. He gave Ruby his card, and suggested that she might enjoy an evening at his restaurant in Berry Street, opposite St. Luke's, the bombed church, the following Friday.

Travelling back in the car, Ruby was impressed, but then she had always been impressed by wealth. Ruby was a schemer. She saw a man with money as another step away from the squalor of her earlier life in a family of ten. Ruby never wanted to work and a succession of 'sugar daddies' had left her fairly solvent with a flat of her own .

She had not been home since she walked out of the house ten years ago, aged fourteen. She did not want to live the rest of her life married to a drunken docker, living in a two-up two-down in Lodge Lane with half-a-dozen screaming kids under her feet. Ruby saw Stavros as the icing on her cake. This could set her up for life and come next Friday she would be accepting his hospitality. Never once did she think she would live to regret it.

Three months later they were married and the 'real' Stavros emerged. He was violently jealous

16

and Ruby was not allowed to show any interest in any other men. He made this plain to her after one week of marriage when he beat her for sharing a joke with one of his waiters. In bed he was rough and only interested in his own satisfaction. He wanted sex on demand, anytime, anywhere. Any protest from Ruby resulted in a slapping. It did not take her long to realise her mistake, but for the moment she was powerless to free herself from her predicament.

The fact that Stavros would be away from Thursday until Monday lunchtime was an enormous relief for Ruby. She was free to go to the Locarno on Friday night and able to meet Billy at the Cygnet looking like a million dollars. She turned the head of every man in the bar.

Her black skirt, split at the side, showed a generous amount of firm, shapely thigh. Her pink sweater was tight and the outline of her breast could be clearly seen. She wore her coat off her shoulder as she glided across the floor towards Billy. There was a low whistle from one of the corner tables and a couple of remarks were passed. This didn't worry Billy. In fact, he regarded it as a compliment; his peers approving of his choice of women. It was music to his ears.

She reached up to Billy and kissed him. Billy ordered a vodka and orange and another Highball.

'We'll have a drink, then make for the Knotty Ash Hotel,' Billy said. 'We can maybe take in one or two other places on the way, if you like.'

'I'm all yours,' Ruby said. You will be, thought Billy, as he took a sip from his drink. He looked at his watch, six thirty, time to call into the Nelson and the Wheatsheaf before getting to the Knotty Ash for eight o'clock. They finished their drinks and, arm in arm, stepped out of the side door into Derby Lane.

4

6.10pm

Stavros was not a happy man. He had telephoned Ruby on Friday evening at seven o'clock. He was pleased that she was at home, but that changed to anger when she said she was going to visit her friend Vera. Stavros raged down the phone that she should stay at home. Ruby, without thinking of the consequences and enjoying her temporary freedom, insisted she was going to visit Vera and put the phone down. She did visit Vera, and Allison, though she omitted to tell Stavros she was 'visiting' them at the Locarno. She did not expect, of course, to meet Billy and had intended coming home at a reasonable hour. The time she was with Billy at the back of the jewellers, meant it was turned one o'clock in the morning when she arrived home. The phone was ringing, and she knew, as she picked it up, that it was Stavros.

'Where have you been?' he screamed down the phone at her and before she had the opportunity to reply he roared again. 'What sort of friends do you have that you stay with them until this time?'

'We had a lot to talk about,' Ruby said calmly, 'I haven't seen Vera for six months and I missed the last bus. I had to wait for a taxi.'

'You had better be telling me the truth,' Stavros

said menacingly. 'Because if I find out you are lying when I get home, I will beat the living crap out of you!'

Ruby was angry with Stavros and in an act of bravado decided she might as well be hung for a sheep as a lamb.

'I will be going out again on Saturday,' she said defiantly. 'For a meal with Vera and Allison.'

Stavros went berserk, spluttering into the phone. 'You little bitch! You will suffer for this!' Then he was screeching. 'Do you hear me? You will suffer for this!'

As his voice faded away, Ruby heard a banging sound. Someone in an adjacent room must be complaining, she thought.

'Fuck you!' she heard Stavros shout and then he was back on the line. 'I'll see you on Monday,' he hissed and slammed the phone down.

Ruby stood shaking for a moment. Well, you've done it now, she thought to herself, so you might as well meet Billy and enjoy the weekend.

All through Saturday's negotiations, Ruby was on Stavros' mind. They broke up at four in the afternoon, arranging to meet up again at eight o'clock for dinner. As soon as he got back to his hotel, Stavros phoned Alex.

'Check her out,' he told him. 'Stay with her. I want to know all her movements over the next two days. You can ring me here until ten to eight. After eight o'clock, I'll be at a restaurant in Soho. I'll get the phone number to you. I would come home now, but it would be considered an insult to my fellow countrymen and I don't want any more trouble than I can handle.'

'Leave it to me, Boss,' Alex said. 'If she's up to no good, I'll deal with it. Any men involved will wish they'd never met her.'

'Good man,' Stavros said. 'But don't forget. Keep me informed.'

A couple of hours later his phone rang. He knew it was Alex and he knew it was trouble.

'It's me, Boss,' Alex said. 'She's just walked into the Cygnet pub in Old Swan.'

'Is she alone?' Stavros asked.

'Yes,' Alex said. 'But, Boss.'

'What?' Stavros demanded, sounding agitated.

'Boss, she's dressed to kill.'

Stavros was deeply disturbed. 'You watch her all the way, Alex,' he ordered. 'For the next two days, you watch her. I want to know where she goes, who she goes with and what she does. Do you understand?'

'Sure, Boss, but I'm going to need help to watch her for two days.'

'OK,' Stavros said. 'Get hold of Nikis. Tell him I'll make it worth his while. And don't use the Humber. She'll recognise it. Ask Nikis to use the Hillman. I'll cover his expenses.'

'Leave it to me, Boss,' Alex said, and put down the phone.

Alex fumbled for change, picked up the receiver and dialled a number. Nikis answered and Alex told him the situation.

'Give me ten minutes,' Nikis said, 'and I'll be

21

there.' Nikis was thrilled at the chance of working someone over. He was always the first to volunteer for this sort of job. As a nasty piece of work, it was right up his street.

Alex, waiting by the phone box opposite the pub, saw Nikis coming along Derby Lane just as Ruby and Billy stepped out of the bar. Lucky for me and unlucky for them, thought Alex, as he walked towards the car. Nikis stopped and leaned across to open the passenger door. Alex got into the car. It was 6-30 p.m.

5

Knotty Ash, Liverpool
7 o'clock

Mrs Walsh pulled on her new leather gloves, a Christmas present from Jack, and listened to Jack telling Bobby not to pick at the buffet.

'Don't have the music too loud, either,' he said firmly. 'And don't have anyone else in the house except Dave. Don't drink more than two bottles of pale ale and don't mess with the guitars!' Tommy and his friend Joe had just tuned them for when they returned from the pub.

'OK, Dad,' Bobby replied, after each 'don't'.

'We'll be home by eleven o'clock,' Mrs Walsh said. 'Make sure the place is tidy. Dave's Ma and dad will be coming in,'

'OK, Ma,'

Jack stepped out through the front door and offered his arm to his wife.

'I think, Queenie, we'll call into the Greyhound for a quickie before going over to the Knotty Ash,' he said.

'Whatever you say,' she said in response. She was just happy to be going out.

As soon as they disappeared from sight, Bobby reached for the volume control on the record player and Chuck Berry's Sweet Little Rock and Roller boomed out.

'Our Billy's bringing his new girlfriend back tonight,' shouted Bobby. 'I hope she's as nice as some of the others.' Bobby's bedroom was over the back door and it wasn't unusual for him to be woken up at one or two o'clock in the morning by Billy and a lady friend leaning against the back door. Bobby learned a lot by looking down on Billy at work.

Across the street, Kate Walsh came out of her friends house with Marie. They had matching candy striped blouses, full skirts, broad belts with large silver buckles, nylons and high heels. That afternoon they had had their hair permed and could have been mistaken for sisters as they made their way up the avenue.

Dave's Ma and dad, Mr and Mrs Tillotson, had already left and soon all would be gathered in the Knotty Ash Hotel. Waiting for them would be Tommy and Betty, and Tommy's mate, Joe, with his girlfriend, Sylvia. The four of them had met in the Greyhound earlier and had taken in one or two local pubs before settling in the Knotty Ash. The talk had centred on Billy and what sort of girl he would have in tow this time. No one expected to meet anyone like Ruby and no one was prepared for the problems she was going to cause them.

Billy and Ruby walked along Prescot Road, through the main shopping area of Old Swan. The shops were closed, but the windows were lit up. It was that time of the evening. The football crowd had gone home and the Saturday night crowd were not yet out in any great numbers. It was fairly quiet.

It was wet underfoot. The pavement glistened in the light from the shop windows. Although it was cold, the air was still. Billy was happy to walk for a while. He lit two Pall Mall and offered one to Ruby. She accepted and drew heavily on it.

'So, tell me about your family,' she said.

'We're just an ordinary lot,' Billy replied. 'Dad's a bit of a taskmaster. What he says usually goes. He had something to do with the unions on the docks before he was injured and had to retire. I know he got into a few scraps when he was a young fella, but he's mellowed a bit now.'

'Have you any brothers or sisters?' Ruby asked.

'Two brothers and one pest of a sister,' Billy said laughing. 'All younger than me. Tommy has just come out of the army. He's a bit like Dad, a bit of a hard case, though he doesn't blow his top as quick as Dad used to. I think the army taught him how to control his aggression, especially when he was fighting the Mau-Mau in Kenya. Then there's Kate, just eighteen and a good-looker. Dad won't be too pleased when the prospective husbands start calling. You'll meet her later. She's coming to the pub. It's her first night out with the family.'

'And what about your other brother,' Ruby persisted.

'That's our Bobby. He's fifteen years old and gets away with murder. It's a different generation. He gets off Scot free with things we didn't even think about doing and all he talks about is Rock n' Roll. Him and his mate, Dave, pester the life out of me to bring them back Little Richard and Chuck Berry records from New York or anything by Buddy Holly or Elvis. I suppose he's a good kid really. He'll run errands for me or wash my shirts, as long as I'm paying. He helps Ma with her Saturday shopping, though I think that's to make sure he gets his Saturday matinee money.'

'It sounds like a really nice family,' Ruby said, with a little sadness in her voice. It was the sort of family she would have liked to have grown up in herself.

Without realising it they had now strolled as far as the Curzon cinema. Suddenly, Billy looked up and saw a bus nearing the stop.

'Come on,' he urged, 'we'll just make it.' They ran the twenty yards or so and skipped onto the rear platform.

'Two to Knotty Ash Station,' Billy said. They sat on the first seat of the lower deck. It was only a two-stop journey. Billy looked out of the rear window as the bus left the stop. He saw the Hillman car pull away from the curb, but took little notice.

Ruby had her head on Billy's shoulder, with her eyes shut. Otherwise, she would have recognised the passenger in the Hillman as it got close to the rear of the bus.

'Pull back,' Alex said.

'OK,' Nikis replied. 'I'm not going fast. It's the bus slowing down for the next stop.'

'Stavros is going to flip when he finds out about this,' Alex said.

'Maybe he's only got himself to blame,' Nikis responded, 'I hear he treats her like shit.'

'That's not our problem,' Alex said. 'Stavros pays my wages, so I do what he says. You'll get a nice little packet out of it, too.'

'I'm not complaining,' Nikis said. 'I just don't understand why someone needs to treat such a beauty so bad.'

'In the four years I've worked for Stavros,' Alex said, 'I've learned very quickly not to try and understand him. I do what he asks and he pays me well.'

'Touché.'

The bus reached the station and Billy and Ruby alighted. They crossed the main road and entered the Nelson pub. Alex left Nikis in the car and followed them. He walked around the back. There was no rear exit. He went to the outdoor sales, bought two bottles of lager and crossed the road back to the car.

'They're in the lounge and there is no rear exit,' he told Nikis. 'Here. Have a lager.'

Nikis took the bottle. The outdoor staff had loosened the tops. Nikis passed Alex a Senior Service cigarette and they lit up.

Twenty minutes later, Nikis tapped Alex on the shoulder.

'Here we go,' he said and started the car.

As Billy and Ruby came out of the Nelson, Ruby was giggling, her coat open. Her pink sweater, pulled tight through her waspie belt, showed off her ample breasts and flat stomach.

Nikis was just about to speak out loud when he thought better of it. You lucky bastard, whoever you are, he thought to himself. When I've finished with you, I'm going to have a little fun with her myself.

They were about to drive off when Billy and Ruby, who had walked about fifty yards, decided to call into the next pub, the Wheatsheaf Inn. Alex told Nikis it was his turn to check it out.

Nikis set off. It was getting colder now and he buttoned up his topcoat as he crossed the road. There were only two entrances. Nikis saw them in the snug. He knew Ruby did not know him. Any work he had done for Stavros in the past had been confidential, so he took a chance and walked into the room. It was small and warm from a coal fire. Apart from Ruby and Billy, there were only three other people in there.

Nikis went up to the bar and ordered a rum and pep. He was close to Ruby and when he heard her laugh, he half turned and saw Billy had his hand on her thigh. He thought he heard Billy ask if she had enjoyed last night. Ruby nodded and giggled.

'Tonight will be a night you won't forget,' he heard Billy say.

Nikis swallowed half of his drink. He felt angry now, knowing he had to go back out into the cold Knowing Billy was going to be doing something he wanted to do himself.

As he finished his drink, he saw Ruby offer her luscious lips to Billy. The kiss said it all. Nikis strode out of the pub and shivered as he got into the car.

'I'm going to enjoy fixing that bastard!' he said to Alex.

6

'Before we meet the family,' Billy said, 'I need to know a few things.'

'Like what?' queried Ruby.

'Like, are you married? And if so, where is your husband?'

'You don't need to know anything other than I'm with you tonight,' Ruby said.

'Ordinarily, I wouldn't be bothered,' Billy said. 'One way or the other. But you fascinate me. I can't stop thinking about you. I've never known another woman like you and now that I've got you, I want to keep you. I need to know if there is a husband waiting for you somewhere.'

So she told Billy a few little white lies. 'My husband is a Greek business man. He spends a lot of time away from home and I get lonely. I don't want you to think I'll go out with anyone, because I don't. I really like you Billy and I'm risking my husband's anger being out tonight.'

'Does he harm you?' Billy asked, concern showing in his voice.

Ruby hesitated for a moment. She did not want to tell Billy how vicious Stavros could be, but she needed to drop a hint, plant a seed in Billy's mind for any future situation.

'He does take off a bit,' Ruby said 'and he has

slapped me once or twice. But I can handle him. He is very jealous, though, and he can be very nasty with any men he sees me talking to.'

He had known at the back of his mind Ruby was married, though he had not bargained for this. 'Fisticuffs' was not Billy's game. He preferred to live by his wits. He was no mug, could look after himself and would not be pushed around, but when it came to the big boys, Billy wasn't in contention.

Stavros sounded like big league to Billy. Perhaps too big. But sitting here next to Ruby he knew he was going to take a chance and he knew he would probably regret it.

'If you want to get out,' Billy said, 'I'll stand by you. I know where we can lie low until the heat's off.'

'The heat would never be off,' Ruby said. 'Stavros would never stop looking for me and even if he doesn't want me back, he'll make sure no one else wants me. He'd take it out on you, too.'

'He doesn't bother me,' Billy lied.

'Oh Billy,' Ruby sighed, 'let's forget about him for now. He won't be home until Monday lunch time. Let's just enjoy the next thirty-six hours. You made me really happy last night. The happiest I've been for almost a year, but come Monday morning, we must go our separate ways.'

'I love you, Ruby,' Billy told her. 'You can't go back to him. I won't let you.'

Ruby was pleased to hear Billy say, 'I love you',

31

but sad at the thought of the consequences. If only she had not danced the tango with him last night.

Billy looked at the clock above the bar. It was 8-05 p.m.

'We must go,' he said. 'They'll all be in the Knotty Ash by now. Drink up.'

Nikis had pulled the car off the main road. It was getting colder as they watched Ruby and Billy, arm in arm, stroll the hundred yards or so to the Knotty Ash Hotel.

Alex was unhappy at having to urinate at the rear of the car, because he could not take a chance and use the pub toilet. Ruby would recognise him. He was hard to miss at six foot tall, blond hair swept back and a distinctive broken nose. He carried a big gut, a result of four years working for Stavros, most of those spent sitting behind a steering wheel or at restaurant tables, eating and drinking.

At thirty-five he had seen two marriages dissolved because of the hours he liked to keep. He liked to sleep all day and be out all night. Illegal gambling was how he made his living. He was quick with his fists, having been a reasonable amateur boxer. It was a natural progression to club doorman and personal bodyguard.

'It looks like we are in for a long wait,' Alex said to Nikis. 'There's a coffee bar on the corner, opposite the village hall. Why don't you walk down and see what you can get? We'll need something hot.'

As he felt like a walk, Nikis agreed to go. He was beginning to stiffen in the cold interior of the car. He walked the two hundred yards to Cappaldi's Cafe, stamping his feet to get some circulation going. He was a smart man and about Billy's age, a second generation Greek. He liked to wear mohair suits, Italian shoes, gold cuff links and matching tie clips. He had his hair trimmed every Saturday morning and the barber always clipped his thin moustache.

Nikis didn't carry any excess weight. He was sinewy with big bony hands, five feet nine inches tall and he could move as quick as a cobra. He had a slight scar along the left side of his chin - the outcome of a flick knife fight when he was a teenager - and black burning eyes. Nikis looked menacing.

He wasn't much of a drinker. Indeed, he wasn't much of a socialiser. When he wasn't working he liked nothing better than to be at home with his young wife and baby daughter, on whom he lavished everything.

Hiring Nikis did not come cheap, but anyone who did always got value for money. He carried out his tasks with cold precision.

With his hands thrust into his coat pockets Nikis walked into Cappaldi's and ordered two coffees and two cheese crumpets to take out. The cafe was busy with teenagers. The jukebox was pounding out What Do You Want by Adam Faith. It was not to Nikis' taste, the whole scene rankled with him. He hastened back to the car. By

33

now he had a real dislike for Billy and he was going to make Billy pay for this uncomfortable Saturday night.

7

8.10pm

The bar in the Knotty Ash Hotel was busy and noisy most Saturday nights and tonight was no exception. It was, perhaps, even noisier, as the Walsh family and friends had swelled the number of patrons. They occupied one side of the bar room and had pulled three or four tables together.

The bar was large, with a fair amount of floor space in the centre. This came in handy for would-be dancers, as music was provided by an elderly harmonica player known as Jock, and his friend, a blind pianist named Harry. They were capable players and there was no shortage of volunteers when it came to giving a song.

Mrs Walsh sat with Kate, Marie, Sylvia and her future daughter-in-law Betty. They sat on the bench seat with their backs to the wall overlooking the bar floor. Jack had supplied them with drinks; port and lemon for Mrs Walsh and lager and lime for the girls. A couple of young lads leaned on the bar looking at Kate and Marie. Jack had noticed them and did not approve. He ventured to the bar for his pint of mild and as he was about to return to his seat he turned to one of them.

'You can look all night, but the moment you make a move, I'll be right behind you.' The two lads spluttered into their beer.

'We're not doing anything wrong, mate,' one of them offered.

'Well, keep doing nothing wrong and we'll all go home happy,' Jack replied and returned to his seat.

Tommy and Joe looked around at the slightly raised voices.

'You all right, Dad?' Tommy asked.

'Just laying down a few guide lines,' Jack said. 'I don't think there's anything to worry about.' The two lads looked at Tommy and Joe and held their hands up in a submissive gesture. Tommy and Joe turned away to concentrate on their drinking.

Some of the regulars came over to say good evening to the family, especially Mrs Walsh, who was rarely seen in the pub. Vinnie and Monica Tillotson joined the company. They had been in the lounge having a chat with friends. The company was now almost complete, except for Billy and his young lady.

Near neighbours, the Molloys, were occupying the opposite corner of the bar. Ada Molloy was the matriarch, a boney woman, sharp featured, with bad teeth. She sidled across the bar floor and squeezed in alongside Mrs Walsh.

'What's the occasion, Queenie?' she asked. 'Must be special for you and your lot to be out.'

Mrs Walsh told her of the belated party and Ada's eyes lit up. Not only might there be a 'do' to go to after closing, but Billy Walsh would be here soon and she thought her daughter Agnes might possibly be Mrs Billy Walsh one day.

36

Agnes Molloy was not Billy's type. She was too thin for a start. Her high cheek bones and mousy hair tied back gave her a harsh look. Billy always thought her mouth was too wide and her feet too big. At every opportunity Ada Molloy had tried to get Billy to ask Agnes out and tonight she would try again.

'Where's that Billy fella?' Jack said. 'He was supposed to be here for eight o'clock.'

'Don't panic, Dad,' Tommy said, 'he's only ten minutes late, he'll be here shortly.'

The bar was filling up now. There was plenty of good-hearted ribaldry and some name calling. The harmonica player and the pianist were playing softly in the background. One of the regulars was taking a spot-the-ball ticket around.

'A shilling a go! Win fifteen bob!' he was shouting. There was no shortage of takers. Fifteen bob was a night's drinking money.

Ada Molloy returned to her seat.

'Guess who's coming in shortly?' she said to Agnes.

'It must be Billy Walsh. He's the only one missing,' Agnes replied. Ada suggested that if they invited him over for a drink, they would probably get an invite back to the Walsh household.

'It's about time you got close to him, Agnes,' she said. 'He's got plenty of money.'

Also with Ada were her two sons. Michael, at twenty-two, was a small weasel-like character, with a pointed nose and big ears. He had a hard mouth with thin lips and deep, staring brown eyes. Michael was a petty thief and a pickpocket. That afternoon he had been to Goodison Park and 'made' a few quid. Tonight he would probably get drunk and say the wrong thing to the wrong person and end up nursing a bloody nose. He didn't get on with anybody, not least his mother. Ada had little time for him. He was always sponging off her and if she refused he would steal it anyway. Ada's favourite was Francis. At thirty, he was the eldest of her three children. She doted on him. They were always together. They went to the cinema and the local bingo, but on a Saturday night they were always in the Knotty Ash Hotel.

Francis had a 'problem', which Ada discovered when he was fifteen. She had gone upstairs to strip the bed for washing. The radio was on loud and Francis did not hear her coming into his room. There she caught him dressed in his sisters knickers and bodice, looking at himself in the mirror. Francis broke down and expected a beating, but Ada loved her boy. She took him in her arms and let him sob, all the time thinking that if only that bastard of a husband had not jumped ship in Australia, maybe the boy would have been different. But she knew that was not true. If Francis was 'queer', she was not going to look for excuses. In the house she let him dress as he pleased. She bought him underwear, shoes, nylons and let him use her make-up. In return, he was fiercely loyal to her.

Francis was enlisted to the RAF for his national service and after two years in Germany he returned a fully-fledged homosexual. He worked as a bus conductor, which allowed him many contacts, and it was not unusual for him to be seen about town with various boyfriends. He looked almost like Agnes' twin. He wore his hair long to his shoulders. This made his face quite feminine. His teeth were white and even and he had a nice smile. He used a little amount of rouge on his sharp features and would have dearly loved to wear eye shadow and lipstick, but Ada would not allow him to go that far in public.

Most of the regulars put up with him, though some passed comments such as 'shirt lifter', 'turd burglar' or 'corn beef inspector'. Most of these comments were passed in hushed tones as Francis was quite fiery and would stand up to anyone taking the 'Mickey'.

Into this scene, at eight-fifteen, walked Billy and Ruby. Billy guided Ruby over to the corner where the family had gathered. There was a sharp intake of breath from Ada and Agnes Molloy as they passed their table.

'Evening everybody,' Billy proclaimed. 'Let me introduce you all to Ruby.'

Tommy and Joe approved instantly. Jack wasn't sure. He would make his mind up when he got to know her better. The girls were delighted, particularly because of Ruby's expensive outfit and her perfect make-up. They wanted to ask her how she did it and where she bought her clothes. It was women's talk and they would love getting to know her.

Ruby leaned over to shake hands with Mrs Walsh. She was being extra polite, but the handshake from Mrs Walsh was curt and quick. She did not like the pain and trouble she saw in Ruby's eyes. She knew Billy had made a mistake. He had made mistakes in the past, of course, but this was going to be a big one. She just knew it.

Ruby sat next to Jack as Billy went to the bar for drinks.

'Our Billy hasn't shut up about you all day,' Jack said. 'You've made quite an impression on him.'

'That's what I'm afraid of,' Ruby said.

'So you don't think it's going to be a long term relationship then?' asked Mrs Walsh.

'I wouldn't put money on it,' Ruby replied. 'We're just enjoying each other's company for the weekend.'

Mrs Walsh hoped it was so. Billy sailed to New York in five days and, once he was away, she hoped he would forget this Ruby.

Billy returned with the drinks, sitting next to Ruby and squeezing her hand,.

'Happy?' he asked.

'Of course,' she answered. 'Your family seem nice, especially the girls. We'll have a chat later.' Billy was just about to peck her on the cheek when Ada Molloy appeared.

'Hello, Billy. This your latest 'Judy' then? I was just saying to our Agnes, fancy Billy Walsh not being in with the family. If he comes in we must ask him to join us for a drink. You remember Agnes don't you, Billy. You used to chat her up at parties. She's still single. Come and have a drink with us. Your 'Judy' wont mind, will she?'

'One,' Billy said; 'she's not my 'Judy', Ada. Her name is Ruby and she's a lady. Two, I don't recall chatting your Agnes up at any party. She's not my type. Three, your Agnes can't dance and, in particular, she can't tango. And four, your Francis is more feminine than her and if he could tango he'd stand more of a chance than Agnes.' With that the whole Walsh family burst out laughing and Ada turned on her heels and stormed back to her seat.

Ada related the humiliation of the conversation to her children.

Michael was furious. He wanted to confront Billy.

'Don't be in any hurry,' said Ada. 'Our day will come. There's more than one way to skin a cat and if I know Billy Walsh, that Ruby whatever-her-name-is will have something to hide. Before the night's out, we'll get even.'

The pianist struck up April Love and Vinnie Tillotson was called upon to sing. Vinnie was a dapper little man, with a slim ginger moustache, and was a good 'phraser'. He went on to sing The Story of my Life and Volare, before making way for one of the female regulars, giving her rendition of Patsy Cline's Crazy.

Things were beginning to warm up. The drink

was flowing and the entertainment was good. Ruby felt happy and relaxed. She had never felt so content. Why couldn't her family have been like this? Why did she hurry into such a bad marriage with Stavros? Why hadn't she met Billy a year earlier? All questions she could not answer and why should she try to answer them now? Why not just enjoy herself for a change.

Billy stood up from his seat. He winked at Ruby and walked across the floor to the pianist.

'Like a drink, Harry?'

'A small rum and water, thanks Billy,' he replied.

'What's yours, Jock?' asked Billy.

'Och, ye ken mine, Billy. A wee dram o' Bells'll do nicely.' Billy ordered the drinks, and as he turned from the bar, Michael Molloy was standing behind him.

'You think you're a smart bastard, Billy Walsh,' he said.

'I'm smarter than you, Michael,' he snapped back. 'But then most people are.' He stepped to one side and passed Michael before he had time to reply. He placed the drinks on top of the piano. 'Do you know The Blue Tango?' he said to Jock

'Sure we do,' said Jock, 'it was a big hit a couple of years ago. Harry and I can play it.'

'Play it nice and tight,' Billy said, 'real sexy and sharp, and there's another drink in it for you.'

'He who pays the piper,' said Jock.

Billy took Ruby by the hand and led her into the middle of the floor. He whispered into her ear.

42

'Make this really sensuous. Erotic even. I want the Molloys to sweat.'

Billy and Ruby swayed across the floor, their bodies locked together, almost moulded. Their steps were sharp, precise, the turns were executed dramatically. People stood up and moved their chairs to allow them freedom to express the dance. With every sharp turn of her head, Ruby's glorious red hair swished and bounced, her eyes sparkled and she felt so sexy she could not believe it. Dancing the tango with Billy Walsh was as good as making love in public.

Billy knew Ruby loved what was happening. He guided her to and fro, across the room, his pelvis thrust into her. He stared into her eyes and he felt the eroticism of the dance getting to him, he was excited. The look of incredulity on the faces of the Molloys spurred him on. He arched Ruby backwards as the music finished and he kissed her. Her thigh was between his legs and he realised he had an erection.

The noise of the regulars brought him back to reality. They were clapping and whistling. Some were thumping the bar. The customers in the lounge had come through and the bar was a heaving mass of cheering people. It took a couple of minutes for the din to die down.

Billy and Ruby returned to their seats and there was still a buzz about the place. People were still talking of the exhibition. The family were congratulating Billy and Ruby, except for Mrs Walsh. As far as she was concerned only the

Devil could make someone dance that like that.

'The Devil knows all the good tunes,' she muttered to no one in particular.

8

8.30pm

Alex had taken a walk around the Knotty Ash Hotel. There were two entrances fronting the main road and one at the side, into the car park. There were only a couple of vehicles in the car park, so they parked the Hillman in the corner adjacent to the neighbouring petrol station. The car and its occupants would not be readily identifiable to anyone leaving the pub, but from the car it was just possible to see the three doorways.

Alex had visited the lounge. He bought some cigarettes and looking through into the bar he saw Billy and Ruby sat with a large group of people. From the look of things they were there for the night, so he left before he was spotted and returned to the car.

'I think this is where we spend the next three hours,' he said to Nikis.

'I was hoping you wouldn't say that,' Nikis replied. 'It's cold enough already and it's getting worse. We're going to be like a couple of icemen before the night is out.'

'I'll have to ring Stavros,' Alex said. 'He said, unless it's urgent, to ring after nine o'clock. They'll have finished eating by then.'

'Well, go and ring him then,' Nikis said.

'Maybe he'll let us go for a kip and catch up with these two in the morning.'

'Somehow, I don't think he will,' sighed Alex, as he walked across to the phone box next to the coffee bar.

'Olympia Restaurant,' the voice said.

'I need to speak to Mr Ziacos,' Alex said. 'Tell him it's long distance from Liverpool. He's expecting the call.' Alex waited.

'That will be another two shillings, sir,' the operator said. Alex inserted the coins, the voice he heard was that of Stavros.

'Well, what's the news?'

'Not good, Boss,' Alex answered, and he went on to tell him of the events of the evening so far. By the time he had finished, he thought Stavros was going to have a heart attack.

Stavros was now a seething maniac. He tried to control his voice, but only with great difficulty. 'You stay with them,' he said to Alex. 'I want this dirty piece of shit who's screwing my wife dealt with. Nikis will make sure he can't do this to any other woman. Then you take Ruby home and you keep her there until I get back on Monday. Do you understand!?'

'Yes Boss,' Alex replied. The operator intervened.

'Another two shillings, sir.' Alex fed in the coins.

'Where can we ring you, Boss?' he asked.

'You can get me here until midnight, then at the hotel. I will tell the night porter I am

46

expecting your call. Make sure the next call you make is better news,' he slammed the phone down.

Alex went into the coffee bar, bought two coffees and two hot dogs and took them back to the car. Nikis was glad to see him, and the hot coffee, too. Alex told him of Stavros' fury and that he wanted some sort of result tonight.

'Leave it to me,' Nikis said. 'I'll go into the pub and see what info I can glean. I think we can take care of this by closing time.' They drank the coffee and Alex had to urinate against the wall. He could not risk going into the pub. Nikis set off for the warmth of the bar, leaving Alex to shiver.

Nikis could not believe his eyes. There was Ruby and Billy dancing so erotically and being cheered on by the patrons. He watched in awe as the dance finished and they kissed. God, he thought, Stavros has lost her.

He ordered a drink and lit a cigarette. Out of the corner of his eye he saw someone looking at him. Was it a girl? He wasn't sure. It looked like a girl, long hair, and what appeared to be make-up, though something told him all wasn't what it seemed. He smiled and raised his glass. Francis smiled back. Francis was delighted. Nikis was just what Francis was looking for. Nikis figured he was queer, but he knew that if he played his hand right, he would learn something to his advantage.

'Come on, Vinnie, give us another song,' shouted Jack. Vinnie Tillotson obliged with South of the Border, after which he encouraged Tommy and Joe. They sang with Singing the Blues, and another Guy Mitchell favourite, The Roving Kind.

Nikis ordered another rum and pep.

'Haven't seen you in here before,' said a voice behind him. He looked round to see Francis fumbling in his purse.

'Allow me,' Nikis said. 'What are you drinking?'

'Bloody Mary, thanks,' Francis said, and then repeated himself. 'Haven't seen you in here before.'

'Just passing,' Nikis lied. 'Needed cigarettes, so I decided to have a quick one while I was here. I couldn't help catching the couple over there, dancing. They're very good. Very sexy.'

'Oh, you mean Billy Walsh and his new girl,' said Francis.

'Is that his family he's with?' asked Nikis.

'That's the Walsh tribe all right,' Francis spat out. 'They think they're too good for us! Billy is a flash, merchant navy stoker. The old man is a nark and that Tommy is a hard knock if he gets upset. An ex soldier, as is his mate, Joe.'

'Who are the girls?' Nikis queried, and Francis, now feeling quite at ease, told him where they lived, at twenty-two Kings Avenue, just down the road, past the rugby ground. That was all he wanted to know. Nikis supplied another Bloody Mary. Francis was enjoying the attention, but he felt he ought to get back to Ada. Nikis let him go and decided to hang around for a while. He might pick up some more useful bits of information.

Half an hour or so went by and Nikis had another rum and pep. He also witnessed various singers and was beginning to tire of it. He decided to use the Gents and then maybe he and Alex could nip down to Kings Avenue, check out number twenty-two and be back before closing.

He moved off to the toilets. He hadn't realised how much he needed to go and he stood at the urinal that long, he failed to notice Francis had joined him. Just as he finished, Francis reached out with his hand.

'Don't put it away,' he breathed. 'Let me hold it. I can really please you.'

Nikis nearly choked with surprise. As swift as a cobra, he seized Francis by the throat and rammed him into a cubical.

'You dirty little faggot!' he snarled.

'But I thought this was what you wanted,' Francis squealed.

'You've made a big mistake, you queer bastard,' Nikis hissed. He held Francis by the throat and put his right hand into his jacket pocket and expertly slipped on a knuckle-duster. The first punch split Francis' nose, the second broke it. Francis screamed and lashed out. His long finger nails caught Nikis on the cheek and drew blood. Nikis grunted. He hit Francis a third time, in the mouth, and burst his lip, breaking two front teeth.

Francis was now sobbing heavily. Nikis slipped

49

the knuckle-duster back into his pocket and then punched Francis three times in the stomach. He took him by the hair and ran him out of the cubical and into the tiled wall of the gents. Francis slid down the wall and lay on the floor coughing and spluttering in blood and vomit. Nikis took out his handkerchief, wet it and dabbed his cheek as he left the toilet. It was all over in less than a minute.

Nikis walked along the passage from the Gents and into the room just as Billy was leaving the bar with a tray of drinks. They nearly collided.

'Careful, pal,' Billy said. Nikis just brushed past him and walked out of the side door.

He crossed the car park to the Hillman and opened the car door. 'Let's go,' he said to Alex. 'Take a right out of the car park and head towards the rugby ground. We're looking for Kings Avenue. It's on the left-hand side of the carriageway. We want number twenty-two.

Alex saw the blood on Nikis' cheek as the interior light came on.

'What happened to you?' he asked.

'I'll tell you about it as we go. I met a damned faggot.'

The car pulled out of the car park, turned right and was gone into the night.

Billy set the tray of drinks on the table.

'I need to go to the Gents,' he told Ruby and he headed for the passage. The door to the gents was difficult to open and he shoved it with his shoulder. The door opened enough for him to put his head around and he gasped at what he saw. Francis had tried to crawl to the door and in doing so had left a trail of blood and vomit. The floor looked a mess and Francis looked worse. Billy bent down

'Francis, what happened? Who did this?'

Francis could not talk. His lips were swollen and his teeth throbbed. He tried to give Billy a description of Nikis, but was unable to. He was still crying and kept reliving the horrifying attack.

Billy took a toilet roll off its holder and wet some of it. He knelt down next to Francis and was just about to clean the blood from his face, when the toilet door opened and in walked Michael Molloy.

9

Mayfair, London
9 o'clock

Stavros Ziacos had heartburn indigestion and a
headache. He was in a foul mood as he splashed
water about his face in the wash room of the
Olympia Restaurant in Brook Street, Mayfair He
reached for the towel and dried himself. He had
taken aspirin and his headache was receding. As
for his heart burn and indigestion, well, he
thought, if I leave the red wine and cigars alone
for a couple of hours they should clear. As he
reached his table, though, he poured himself
another drink and lit a half- corona.

'You OK, Stavros?' asked Kris, his host.

'Yeah, yeah,' Stavros replied. 'Just a bit of
bother in Liverpool. My boys are taking care of it,
but I'll be happy to get home, just the same.'

'Don't worry,' said Kris. 'Things will work out
just fine. And when you go back to Liverpool on
Monday, you will be a very rich man. This is a
good deal,' he added. 'Worth taking time over.'

Milo, from Birmingham, suggested another
bottle of wine. 'Now we have more or less agreed
the deal, let's see how quickly the lawyers can
write it up to-morrow. If everything is to your
satisfaction, there's no reason why you should not
take the train on Sunday evening.'

Stavros perked up at this suggestion. 'A good idea,' he said, and raised his glass. His headache was now a distant memory. He took a deep drag on his cigar and blew a large trail of smoke into the air. 'Yes, more wine,' he said loudly.

Kris leaned forward and gestured the other two move closer to him. 'Now we are agreed amongst ourselves, I thought you might like to relax for a couple of hours. I've arranged for a few friendly girls to drop in shortly. There are rooms available upstairs.'

Milo and Stavros looked at each other, smiling.

'That's a nice touch, Kris,' said Milo. 'Don't you agree, Stavros?'

'A very nice touch,' Stavros agreed. 'Now where's that wine?'

Things were not looking so black after all. He had a good deal. Added to his existing three restaurants, was one in Manchester. Kris had four across London and Milo had two in Birmingham and was looking to acquire others in Nottingham and Derby. By pooling resources and buying centrally, their profits would go up and their expenses down. They were going to be very rich men, so why let the red haired slut in Liverpool spoil it, he thought, as he put his arm around the waist of the small blonde who had just appeared. He directed her to the stairs.

As he passed the table, he picked up a bottle of wine and two glasses. Might as well enjoy myself, he thought. No reason why Ruby should have all the fun. Yet as soon as he said her name to himself, the pang hit him in the pit of his stomach like a bayonet. He knew he was the loser. It didn't matter who he bedded. The fact that someone other than himself would be making love to Ruby tore through him.

He shoved the blonde roughly up the stairs.

'Don't delay getting stripped off,' he told her, then shouted back to Kris, 'Tell your man on Reception where I am. I'm waiting for an important call from Liverpool. He must put it through to me.'

Stavros suddenly felt foul again. As they entered the room, he pushed the girl onto the bed. 'Come on, come on!' he snarled. 'Get out of those clothes!' The girl hurriedly stepped out of her skirt as Stavros poured himself a glass of wine. He unbuckled his belt and let his trousers drop. He kicked them from around his feet and took off his shorts. The girl was unhooking her bra when Stavros hit her. 'Come on, come on!' he said again. 'On your knees! On the bed!'

'But I don't like it that way . . . ' She hardly had the words out when Stavros hit her again.

'But I do,' he said, 'and you are not here for what you like, you are here for what I like. So bend over!'

Stavros was particularly well-endowed and he was always aroused when he was in control. He took another gulp of wine and, still standing up, entered the girl from behind. He was rough. He pulled her nipples and pummelled her breasts and buttocks. It didn't take long for him to reach a

54

climax. The girl experienced only humiliation.

When he finished, he lit a cigar.

The girl asked could she get dressed.

'No, stay where you are,' Stavros said. 'I will need you again.'

There was a knock on the door.

'Yes,' he said.

'A phone call for you, Mr Ziacos. Long distance.'

'I'm on my way down.' Stavros replied. He dressed quickly and turned to the girl.. 'Stay put and help yourself to a drink. I might have something to celebrate when I return.' Then he was gone.

The girl began to tremble and cry.

10

Knotty Ash, Liverpool
9 o'clock

Michael Molloy screamed at Billy. 'You mean bastard! You sly piece of shit!' He kicked out, hoping to catch Billy before he could stand up, but Billy was too quick. He dodged the blow and was on his feet before Michael regained his balance. Billy grabbed Michael by his lapels and swung him against the wall. He slapped his face and told Michael to shut up and listen.

'I didn't do this!' he said. 'Look at me. I don't have any blood on me and my hands are not marked. This is a professional job. Go into the bar and ring for an ambulance and the police. I'm not into this sort of violence, but so help me God, Michael, if you ever threaten me again, I'll kick the shit out of you! Understood?'

'OK, Billy,' Michael replied. 'You must admit, it did look suspicious. How's Francis, anyway?'

'He'll survive,' Billy said, 'but his looks will suffer. I think his nose is broken. Tell your mother to come through and bring some bar towels with her. Now hurry it up!'

Ada Molloy, clutching the bar towels, ran screaming to the gents. She was followed by Agnes, Michael and most of the customers in the bar. The story soon circulated to the rest of the pub and quite a few people said they noticed Francis talking to a good looking, smartly dressed man. The barmaid in particular, remembered him.

'He could have been Greek or Turkish,' she told the manager.

By now the local bobby had arrived on his Vespa motor scooter. This had succeeded the policeman's bike and enabled him to cover a larger beat quicker.

Constable Bertram Drummond was nicknamed 'Bulldog', not because he solved cases with the same devil-may-care manner of the British screen hero of the same name, but because his lower jaw protruded out from his upper jaw and, as he was overweight and slightly bow legged, it was natural that he would acquire such a nick name.

Constable Drummond was no stranger to Billy and Tommy Walsh. He had booked Billy a couple of times for being drunk and disorderly and he had locked Tommy up in the local cells for fighting. He was a frequent visitor at the Molloys to 'speak to Michael'. He knew what people called him, and he ignored the whispered 'it's Bulldog' and pushed his way through the crowd in the passage.

'Come on now, get back to your drinking. Make some space here!' he shouted. 'Move yourselves. I only want people here who saw something. Come on, move yourselves!'

The crowd thinned. Although people liked to mock Bulldog, they would only do it behind his back. He was a tough nut, and as most of the local hard cases would testify, he could look after himself.

'Last time of asking, folks,' he shouted. 'If you weren't involved, go away. I'll speak to you all later.'

The hangers-on, after getting a glimpse of the battered Francis, drifted away.

The ambulance arrived and one of the two ambulancemen in attendance cleaned Francis up. 'You will have to go to hospital, son. Looks like a broken nose. And your lip will need stitching, as will the head wound.'

Francis was shaking. The thought of having his nose set and having stitches was as bad as the beating.

'What happened?' Drummond asked.

Francis told him as best he could what Nikis had done.

'So where do you come in?' he asked Billy.

'I found him here, Bull . . . , er, I mean constable,' Billy replied.

'Did you see anyone?'

'Now that you ask,' Billy said, 'I was carrying a tray of drinks from the bar when this guy pushed past me, nearly knocking the tray out of my hand. He was tall, well dressed and dark. Mediterranean type. Don't know if I would recognise him again though. I was more concerned with saving the drinks. When I looked up, he was gone.'

Agnes, who had been crying, said she saw Francis at the bar with someone fitting that description. She had not seen him in the pub before.

Ada was furious.

'If you've got anything to do with this, Billy Walsh, I'll swing for you,' she snarled.

'Don't take off on me, Ada,' Billy warned. 'Why would I want to see Francis hurt. He's never harmed me.'

The ambulancemen were ready to take Francis to hospital.

Ada and Agnes were going with him, but Michael elected to stay. He wanted to keep an eye on Billy. He would still like to get something on him, if only because he didn't like him.

Drummond checked Ada's address and said he would call the next day for statements and then went off to the bar to talk to any would-be witnesses, particularly the barmaid. Most people had resumed their drinking and Harry was quietly tinkling the piano as Billy came back and sat next to Ruby.

'Everything OK now, Billy?' she asked.

'Yeah, nothing to worry about,' he replied. 'Francis must have tried his hand with the wrong fella. The police have got a description. They'll probably pick him up before long. He's bound to have some blood on him.'

He did not mention to Ruby that the man had asked Francis about him. No point in unduly worrying her, he thought. Not while she was enjoying herself.

Ruby had heard the talk in the bar. Indeed, it

had reached everyone's ears and the girls were repeating what they had heard. Possibly a Greek or Turkish man, definitely from somewhere in the Mediterranean. This worried Ruby, though for Billy's sake she tried not to show it.

Mrs Walsh, however, noticed Ruby's concern straight away.

'Billy,' she said, 'if your young lady is upset, get a taxi and take her home.'

'She's OK Ma,' Billy said. 'She's coming home with us and we're going to have a knees- up and a good sing-song.'

Just what I feared, thought Queenie Walsh. She moved to sit by Jack. 'Don't let the boys get into trouble over this, Jack,' she demanded.

'It's nothing to do with us, Mother,' Jack answered. 'And there won't be any trouble from us if we're left alone.'

Mrs Walsh glanced at Ruby. She could see she was still perturbed. She knew this had something to do with her and that it wasn't over yet.

The patrons had settled down again and Vinnie Tillotson had them all singing,

'There's a Pawnshop on the Corner,
In Pittsburgh, Pennsylvania.'

Ruby had relaxed a little and was singing along with Billy when a hand tapped him on the shoulder.

11

9.30pm

Alex and Nikis saw the policeman on his Vespa motorscooter on the other side of the carriageway, heading in the direction from which they had just come. Concentrating on reaching his call as swiftly as possible, he had no reason to notice the black Hillman as it slowed down to turn left into Kings Avenue.

'Number twenty-two is on the right,' Nikis said. 'Slow down or you'll miss it.'

'This is it, by the street lamp,' Alex pointed. 'I think I'll reverse into the side street and we can walk round. No point in letting anyone see the car.' He reversed into Maidford Road and parked by the school gates. 'There are only houses on one side of the road, so there shouldn't be too many nosy bastards,' he said.

It was colder now and slippery underfoot. The wind had picked up slightly and brought with it a smattering of snowflakes. Nikis and Alex put on their trilbies and turned up their coat collars as they left the car and made their way round the corner into Kings Avenue. The avenue was deserted. Most of the houses had their curtains drawn. Nikis envied the occupants, who were probably snuggled in armchairs, watching Dragnet or Wagon Train on the television.

They reached number twenty-two.

'It's a bit noisy,' Alex said, as he lifted the latch on the gate.

'You can say that again,' Nikis agreed.

As they reached the door, they could clearly hear Little Richard belting out Long Tall Sally. There was an entry between numbers twenty-two and twenty, where the Tillotsons lived.

Alex suggested they take a look up the entry. They reached the top and tried the doors giving access to the back gardens. Both were open. Alex went into the rear of twenty-two and Nikis went into the rear of number twenty. Nikis could hear the faint sound of the Tillotsons TV set as he checked the rear garden. At the bottom of the garden, he could see the school fence and the playing field.

Alex walked into the rear garden of number twenty-two. He heard a clucking sound and was just about to step into the garden area when the kitchen light came on. He quickly stepped back into the shadows and took stock of what he could see. In the centre of the garden was a large chicken coop and, from the noise they were now making, he guessed there must have been a dozen or more birds in there.

Running up the side of the garden was what appeared to be a long low rabbit hutch. Between the hutch and the coop, Alex could just make out rows of tilled earth. Looks like their vegetable patch, he thought.

He edged forward to see if he could get a glimpse

through the window and he saw Bobby and Dave pouring a bottle of beer. They looked like they were enjoying themselves. He could just make out the prepared buffet on the kitchen table. Suddenly, the record changed to Chuck Berry's Sweet Little Sixteen and the boys were singing along.

Alex backed out into the entry and met up again with Nikis.

'What do you think?' Nikis asked.

'I think there's going to be a party here, and I think this Billy fella will be coming back here from the pub with Ruby. We should be able to take care of things for Mr Ziacos quite nicely.'

They returned to the car and Nikis pointed out that the gardens backed onto the school fence. They would be able to gain access from the rear, if need be.

Alex decided that they should phone Stavros and put him at ease. Let him know that the job is all but sorted and that by Sunday morning it would be complete. They drove to the top of Kings Avenue and found a call box. Alex inserted the coins and gave the operator the number.

'Yeah, yeah,' said Stavros, 'I hope this is good news.'

Alex updated Stavros, but omitted Nikis' fracas in the Knotty Ash pub.

'So you see, Boss, he's got to come back to the house and he's got to leave with her sometime and we'll be waiting. You enjoy yourself tonight and I'll ring you at the hotel in the morning when it's all over.'

'Don't let me down now, Alex,' Stavros said sternly. 'I'll be looking forward to that call.' Stavros put the phone down a happier man. He collected another bottle of wine and returned upstairs. The girl, still snivelling as he entered the room, covered herself with the sheet.

'Now then, don't be embarrassed,' boomed Stavros, as he pulled the sheet away from her. 'I've just had some good news,' he said, 'and I like to share my good fortunes. Here.' He reached into his pocket. 'A little something for you.' He threw two ten pound notes onto the bed.

She could not believe it. Twenty pounds was more than she could earn in a week. She brightened up and Stavros slipped out of his trousers, poured himself another glass of wine and sat on the bed. He pulled the girl roughly to him.

'Now where were we,' he said.

12

Knotty Ash, Liverpool
9.30pm

Billy spun round as the hand clapped him on the shoulder,

'What the — ' was all he got out, then with a smile. 'Oh, it's you Vic,' he said.

'Watcha, Billy!' Vic's cockney accent was as strong as ever despite his years in Liverpool. He had served with Billy on a number of ships and he and Billy had become good friends.

Vic had met a girl in Liverpool and decided to leave the sea, marry her and settle down. He had saved a small fortune over a couple of years while working as a bar steward. On Vic's last trip the girl ran off with a Petty Officer in the Royal Navy, whom she subsequently married, and now lived in Plymouth. Vic Scott was devastated, but determined to carry on with his plan, which was buying and selling used cars.

Vic had noticed the increasing popularity of the car and the subsequent demand for second-hand vehicles. He had invested in a piece of land behind the Knotty Ash village hall two years ago and had established himself.

He never quite got over losing Monica, to a Royal Navy lad of all people, and had not hurried into another relationship. He now lived alone in a flat above the barber's shop in the middle of a row of shops just along the road from the Knotty Ash Hotel.

It was just what he wanted. From his front window he could look down each morning on his car lot. He knew he had done well and it would not be long before he could afford a smart house. Somewhere out of town.

The down side to that was having a drink with Billy and one or two of the other boys he used to sail with less often. He always looked forward to hearing that Billy Walsh was home. He liked Billy's company and he was pleased when Billy had called in to the lot to see him on the Friday afternoon. Billy told him about the party and Vic assured him he would come.

'As soon as I've secured everything and stowed the paperwork,' he said.

Vic was a garrulous type, five foot eight inches in height, with black, wavy hair. He had a pleasant smile, with very even, white teeth. He liked to wear drape jackets, with a link button, and he always wore a dickey bow, a legacy of his bar-tending days.

Ruby moved to sit with the girls for a while and was immersed in discussing make up and hair dressing. The girls were admiring her clothes. Vic noticed her and he let out a low whistle.

'Who's the red head?' he queried.

'Oh, that's Ruby. She's with me,' Billy answered. 'I met her last night at the Locarno. She's some dancer.'

'Don't tell me she can tango. You sure know how to pick 'em. Good looks, good figure, long legs and she can tango. You're a lucky devil, Billy Walsh.'

Billy grinned. He knew most of the men in the pub would agree with Vic. Then Vic asked the question he always asked.

'Is she married?'

Billy told Vic about Stavros and Vic nearly choked on his beer.

'Billy,' he said. 'Hold it, hold it. Does this geezer live on the other side of Old Swan?'

'Yeah, why?' answered Billy.

Vic moved closer to Billy and dropped his voice.

'I know the geezer. Not personally you understand, but you know the Barlow's garage and car sales place on the corner of East Prescot Road and Queens Drive?'

'Yeah. What's that got to do with Ruby?' Billy was concerned.

'Listen to me, Billy,' Vic said. 'I heard about this Greek geezer from Old Swan who buys a used Vauxhall Velox for his old lady off this Barlow geezer. Pays him three hundred pounds cash. A week later, the Vauxhall breaks down.' Vic lifted his glass to his lips and then carried on. 'The Greek says to Barlow, "Sort it out!" The Barlow geezer has the car brought in, examines it, but finds nothing wrong with it. The Greek and his old lady show up for the car and Barlow tells them, "There's nothing wrong with the vehicle, gov'nor. Might I suggest that your trouble and strife is not fully acquainted with the idiosyncrasies of the internal combustion engine in particular and the motor vehicle in general." Well,' Vic paused and looked closely at Billy.

'Apparently this Greek geezer explodes,' he continued. 'He hits Barlow that hard he puts out two of his front teeth and knocks him over his counter. While Barlow is out on the deck, the Greek picks up a wheel brace and starts wrecking the place. A couple of mechanics come running over, but and he threatens them with any kind of violence they think they can handle. But they only work there, don't they, so they back off. He leans over the counter and spits on Barlow, dropping the keys on his head. "Keep the car," he says to him, "and make sure I've got my three hundred pounds back by noon to-morrow!' He bundles his old lady into his car and drives off.'

Vic looked at Billy to see if the story was having the desired effect on him. 'Now you're telling me, Billy, that you and this red haired vision of beauty, who just happens to be Mrs Greek geezer, have been dancing the tango!?'

Billy looked at Vic. He tried to sound calm, but his heart rate had quickened and his stomach had tightened.

'You're not having me on, are you Vic?'

'I'm not telling pork pies,' Vic replied. 'And it looks like this woman means more to you than a one-night-stand.'

'She sure does,' Billy said. 'We've done more

68

than dance the tango.' Billy then told Vic what happened to Francis Molloy and the description of the attacker.

'I think you'd better watch your back,' Vic advised. 'You should tell Tommy and Joe. Tommy is a match for most.'

'I'll have a quiet word with them,' Billy said. 'I don't want to worry Ma or Ruby.' He glanced across at Vic, his smile back in place. 'Now that you're here, though, you could do me a favour.'

'Shoot,' said Vic.

'If you're coming back to ours for a drink, how about you lend me your place tonight. You can kip on our couch.'

Vic slipped his keys to Billy, returning the grin. 'You haven't heard a word I've just said, have you? The back door from the entry's open. Make sure nobody's watching you.' He slapped Billy across the arm. 'Enjoy yourself, but don't get in too deep.'

'I think I already am,' Billy replied. 'Anyway, let's get you another drink and you can give us one of your cockney songs – Knock 'em in the Old Kent Road. That should get them all singing.' Billy went to the bar and ordered a round of drinks.

Ruby joined him and kissed him on the cheek.

'You OK now?' Billy asked.

'I'm all right,' Ruby said. 'I don't think it's anything to worry about. The girls are sure that it was just a stranger passing through and Francis thought he was on.'

Billy passed the drinks round and then sat by Ruby. They were watching Vic giving a song.

Ruby said, 'Your family and friends are lovely people. I wish I had people like this around me. It's so close and happy. I really envy you.'

'You can have this, Ruby, if you stay with me. We'll look after you. Money and fancy trappings aren't everything you know. Peace of mind counts for a lot and I can give you that.'

'I know you can, Billy,' she sighed, 'and the longer I'm with you, the more I want to stay. But I don't want you hurt.'

'I'm not going to get hurt. I'm Billy Walsh, the great survivor.' He touched her cheek and kissed her on her nose. Out of the corner of his eye he saw a look of disapproval on his mother's face and it saddened him.

He drew Ruby to him and whispering, he told her about having the use of Vic's place for the night.

Ruby gripped his hand. 'Oh Billy! You naughty, naughty, clever boy!' She breathed into his ear. 'Let's not waste time going back to your house. Why don't we go straight to Vic's when the pub closes?' Her response could not have pleased Billy more.

'If that's what you want, it's OK by me,' he said. 'By the way, did you ever own a Vauxhall Velox?'

'Stavros bought me a car, though I don't know what make it was. Anyway, it didn't work, so Stavros took it back. Why do you ask?'

'No reason,' Billy said. 'I just thought I heard you mention to the girls you once had a car. Anyway, it doesn't matter.' Billy knew he wanted to taste the forbidden fruit, but he knew he would have to be careful. Otherwise, the price might be high.

13

Mayfair, London
10 o'clock

Stavros shook hands with Kris and Milo. He was a happier man now that Alex and Nikis were on top of things. Now that he knew whoever this guy was with Ruby, would soon be dealt with severely.

The waiter came into the room.

'Your taxi is here, Mr Ziacos.'

'OK, let's go,' Stavros ordered. He gripped the blonde by the arm and propelled her towards the door leading to the street outside the restaurant, making his farewells to his two compatriots. 'See you to-morrow afternoon, two o'clock.' He was hoping the lawyers would have everything ready for signing by late afternoon. Then perhaps he could catch the evening train back to Liverpool.

'We will proceed as quickly and as prudently as possible,' Kris said. 'In the meantime, enjoy the rest of your night. We'll pass on any phone calls.'

The girl climbed into the cab and Stavros followed.

'Hamilton Hotel, Piccadilly,' he said. He sat next to the girl and put his hand on her thigh. He let it creep up. She had left her knickers off, as he demanded, and she opened her legs obediently. He reached for her hand and put it on his lap.

She unzipped his fly and her fingers felt his enormous size, erect again. Oh God, she thought, he is insatiable! He loves needed to be in control and the fact that they were in the back of a cab only made it more exciting for him.

Still, she thought, just get through the night. He had given her twenty pounds and there was a promise of another twenty. This was good money, too good to turn down. It would take her a lot longer than a week as a bar hostess to earn twenty pounds.

He had already had her twice and now he was erect again and wanting a hand job in a cab. Surely he couldn't keep this going all night, she thought. She had never known anyone like him. Little did she know how hard it was going to be to earn her money.

Agnes and Ada Molloy were in the waiting room at Broadgreen Hospital. The doctor had told them of the extent of the injuries Francis had suffered. His nose was reset, but it would never be straight again and he would need dental treatment as soon as the swelling went down. They had stitched him up and sedated him, so there was no point in Agnes or Ada hanging around. What Francis needed was rest. When they came back on Sunday there would be an improvement. Reluctantly, they decided to leave and go home.

'I'm going to see that Billy Walsh,' said Ada. 'I'm convinced this has something to do with him.

Francis will tell me to-morrow and if my suspicions are proven, I'll have that taken care of.'

'You've got no proof, Ma,' Agnes protested. 'It could be a coincidence. Don't act too hastily.'

'Our Francis will supply all the proof I need,' Ada hissed. 'Let's get home. Looks like we won't be going to any party at the Walshes after all.'

They left the waiting room and walked through the hospital grounds to the exit. All the time, Ada was talking about the man at the bar.

'He bought Francis two Bloody Marys. He must have been after something.'

Agnes guided them to the bus stop, but Ada declined, saying she would rather walk. 'It's only twenty minutes or so and I need to think.'

They turned into Brookside Avenue, a long straight road. The air was crisp and the ground frosty, but Ada didn't notice either. She was scheming her revenge.

At the bottom of Brookside Avenue, they came to the roundabout on East Prescot Road. They were about to cross the road and head towards the rugby ground, when they heard a noise to their left. Looking up the road, some hundred yards or so, was the Knotty Ash Hotel. A crowd had spilled out onto the pavement. There was plenty of laughter and people were wishing each other good-night. Some of the Walsh crowd were carrying crates of ale. They all look happy now, thought Ada, but they'll regret what happened to my Francis. Every dog has it's day.

14

10.15pm

'Come on folks, drink up. Let's be having you then.' Austin, the barman, was shouting and although the music had ceased, little groups of people were still singing, Heart of My Heart and Barefoot Days. Some still had a couple of pints left to sink.

Eugene, the manager, was now involved. 'Drink up, boys and girls. You can talk outside.'

The barmaids were trying to clear the tables and empty the ashtrays. The Walsh family were putting on their coats and preparing to leave.

Billy approached his mother. 'Ruby won't be coming back to the house, Ma,' he said, 'I'll be taking her home.' Least Ma knows the better, he thought.

'OK, son,' Mrs Walsh replied. 'I don't dislike Ruby ,you know. I just feel that she's not the right sort for you. You make sure you get back home as soon as you can. Have you got taxi money?'

'Of course I have Ma,' Billy replied. 'I'll see you later.'

While the girls were preparing to leave. Tommy and Joe were stood at the bar finishing their drinks.

Billy approached them. 'Listen, fellas,' he said, 'Vic has given me the key to his flat above the barbers. Ruby and I are going there now. I've told Ma I'm taking her home and I'll be back shortly, so don't be too alarmed if you don't see me until to-morrow sometime. Sorry to duck out of the do.'

'Make hay,' said Tommy. 'I'll keep Ma sweet.'

'You lucky bleeder,' said Joe. 'I'd do the same if I were in your shoes.'

Michael Molloy was rolling a cigarette and ready to head off home, when he heard Billy explaining to Tommy and Joe where he was taking Ruby. Michael took his time and slowly drained his glass. He got the full story, lit his smoke and stepped out into the street. Vinnie Tillotson and Vic Scott were already outside the pub, preparing to carry a crate of beer. Michael bade them good-night and set off. It was then he saw his mother and Agnes waiting to cross the road at the round-about. Michael jogged towards them.

'How's Francis?' he asked.

'He'll be OK,' Agnes replied, 'though he'll look rough for a while and he'll need a couple of false teeth.'

Ada Molloy snarled.

'It should have been that bastard Billy Walsh who got the beating, not my Francis.'

'Oh, he's off for the night with Miss World,' Michael said, 'staying at Vic's flat above the barber's. I heard him telling Tommy and Joe not to expect him home until to-morrow sometime.'

'Well, well, well,' Ada muttered. 'You sure about that, Michael?'

'Yes, Ma. Vic has given Billy his key.'

'Well, well, well,' Ada muttered again. Suddenly she felt a little better.

Alex decided to take a walk. His toes were freezing and a walk would get his blood circulating again.

'Don't go too far,' Nikis said, 'and don't bump into Ruby.'

'I won't,' Alex replied, and he set off. He turned into Kings Avenue, stamping his feet as he walked. It was less than a hundred yards to the top of the avenue and as he reached it, he was beginning to feel his toes again. He stood on the corner and lit a cigarette. Looking to his right, he could see a couple of groups of people heading in his direction. He watched for a moment. The first was a group of three, huddled together, talking intently. Some yards behind them came two men carrying a crate of beer and further behind came a large group, talking loudly, laughing and singing.

It was a clear night and the street lighting illuminated the scene well. Alex could not see Ruby among any of the groupings and Alex knew instinctively she was not there. With her height, her dress, her hair, she would be obvious in any company and she wasn't there. Oh shit, thought Alex. What do we do now? He ground out his cigarette as the trio reached him. He took a chance.

'Excuse me,' he said, touching his trilby.

'Yes?' Ada Molloy grunted.

'I'm looking for Billy Walsh,' Alex said. 'I've been to his address, but he's not at home. I wonder if you might have seen him tonight?'

'You from the shipping company or the police?' Michael asked.

'Oh, the shipping company,' Alex quickly replied. He realised the others were closing, so he turned into the avenue and the Molloys' followed him.

'Is he in lumber then?' Ada queried.

'Could be, if we don't get hold of him soon.'

'I might have some useful information,' said Ada, 'but it'll cost you.' Ada thought, if I can put a stop to your good time tonight, Billy Walsh, and make a few quid to boot, then that will go some way to getting even over Francis.

They reached Ada's front gate on the corner of the avenue. Alex reached into his inside pocket, pulled out his wallet and extracted a five pound note.

'Is that it?' said Ada.

'Take it, or leave it,' was Alex's reply. Ada hesitated for just a moment, then she snatched the note,

'Tell him what you know,' she snarled at Michael. Michael told Alex what he had overheard at the bar. He also told him where the barber's shop was and of the little entry alongside. Michael knew his way around the area, having burgled one or two of the premises. Alex tipped his hat and thanked the Molloys. As he turned away, he watched the crowd going up the path of the Walsh house some doors away, still singing and laughing. As the door opened he could hear Fats Domino, belting out Blueberry Hill. Hope you all enjoy yourselves, he thought, because I will.

He walked round the corner into Maidford Road and got into the car.

'I think we have got ourselves a result,' he beamed at Nikis. 'Let's go back to the Knotty Ash Hotel. We'll leave the car in the car park, then have a stroll to the barber's.'

Nikis looked at him. 'You sure the cold hasn't numbed your brain. We don't need haircuts at this time of night.'

'You're right, Nikis, but I know someone who is going to have a very close shave. Now let's go!'

15

10.15pm

Billy guided Ruby into the entry. On the right side he found the door. As Vic had promised, it was not locked. He lifted the latch and opened it. On the right were a set of metal stairs leading to a veranda which ran the length of the shops. The front door to each shop flat led onto the veranda.

'That's Vic's flat,' whispered Billy, pointing to the door at the head of the stairs.

'Oh Billy, let's get inside and make ourselves comfy.' Ruby was half giggling as she said this. She was excited and nervous.

'Not too much noise,' Billy warned. 'We don't want to alert Vic's neighbours.'

Billy opened the door and found the light switch. There was a long passage into a large front room. Billy had never been in Vic's flat before, so he looked around to acquaint himself. The first door on the left was the bathroom and toilet, the door on the right led to Vic's small but neat kitchen.

'Tea or coffee?' Billy shouted.

'Coffee for me,' Ruby said. She had found her way into the large front sitting room, removed her coat and switched on the electric fire.

Billy put the coffee in the cups. He was feeling pleased. He rubbed his hands together and was whistling Baby It's Cold Outside as he found the door and negotiated his way up the stairs to Vic's attic bedroom. He pulled on the light cord at the top of the stairs to reveal a double bed. Well done, Vic, he thought. The room was quite cosy with a small electric fire under the window. Billy turned on just one bar, enough to take the chill off the room. He was excited now. He was looking forward to the next few hours.

He hurried down to the kitchen to make the coffee. A hot drink and a couple of scotch should just about do it, he thought. A bit of fun on Vic's couch, a bit of teasing, then up to that big bed. Good old Vic! He must have bought the double bed for when he and Monica were married. Looks like she never used it. Billy resolved to do it justice. Good old Vic, he thought again.

He made the coffee and carried it into the front room. Ruby was sat on the carpet in front of the fire. She looked quite sensual, her red hair falling over her shoulders. There was a glow about her face. Her mouth was slightly open and she sat on her legs so that her skirt had ridden up over her thighs. Billy noticed her legs were bare, she must have taken her nylons off while he was looking around the flat.

He suddenly wanted her, there and then, but he controlled himself and passed her a coffee.

'Would you like a scotch with that?' he asked.

'Just a small one, and some water,' Ruby said. Billy went into the kitchen and found a couple of glasses. He poured two scotch, a small one with water, and a reasonable measure for himself. This should be just enough. Don't want brewers droop, he muttered to himself.

He sat by Ruby.

'This is nice,' he said.

'Don't talk too much now,' Ruby said, 'Let's drink our coffee and take our scotch to bed. I want you to love me tonight like it's the end of the world. I want all of you until you can't give any more. I want you so very much.' She leant forward and kissed him.

Billy's temples were pounding. He realised his hand holding the coffee cup was shaking.

'I'll give you all you ever wanted, and more,' he told her. They drank their coffee and made their way upstairs. Billy walked across the room and closed the curtains. He groped his way back and pulled the light cord.

'On or off?' he asked.

'On, of course,' giggled Ruby. 'But let me go to the bathroom first to freshen up. I won't be long.'

Alex saw the sitting room light go off and seconds later the attic light go on. 'That's where they are,' he said to Nikis. 'Looks like they're there for the night.'

'Shall we pay them a visit now?' suggested Nikis.

'Not just yet,' Alex said. 'It's too early. The neighbours are still up and there are still some people around at the chip shop and the cafe. It's too risky. We may get spotted. We can, with some certainty, assume they'll be there for a while. After they finish playing around and screwing, they'll probably sleep like tops. I don't think we should worry about it for the next few hours.'

'What do you say we go to Stavros' house. It's only a few minutes away. We can get something to eat, clean up and have a kip in the warmth. If we come back about five o'clock when Mr Billy Walsh is in dreamland, he won't know what's hit him.'

Nikis thought for a moment. He knew Alex was talking sense, but he did not want to come back and find the bird had flown.

'You take the rap if he's gone when we get back. You hold your hands up to Stavros.'

'No problem,' Alex said.

'Let's go then,' Nikis said. 'I could do with getting the cold out of my bones and a bit of kip. I hope the Tango Kid enjoys himself, because he won't be able to after to-morrow morning.'

16

11 o'clock

Billy walked over to the small bay bedroom window and, as he pulled the curtains closed, he noticed the Hillman car pull out of the Knotty Ash Hotel car park and drive past the flat in the direction of Old Swan. To Billy it was just another driver making his way home.

He also noticed it was snowing lightly. He hoped it did not stick, but he felt good knowing he was inside and warm and that Ruby was waiting for him.

The small electric fire had done its job. The room was cosy. He turned away from the window and lit a Pall Mall as Ruby returned from the bathroom. She had found one of Vic's bathrobes, but had not bothered to tie it up. Billy gasped when he saw her. Her breasts were large and firm and her stomach flat. There was a small triangle of hair at the top of her legs, legs that were long and smooth, almost athletic.

She smiled at Billy. 'You're not disappointed then?' she murmured.

'You could not disappoint me,' Billy replied. He passed her the half-smoked cigarette, 'I'll just go and use Vic's toothbrush,' he said.

That will make two of us,' Ruby answered. 'Do you think Vic will mind?'

'No. I'll get him a box of toothbrushes first thing Monday morning. A favour like this is worth at least a box of toothbrushes.' Billy pointed to the unit at the bedside. 'There's a small radio on the bedside cabinet. See if you can get some music on while I'm away.'

'Don't be long, Billy,' Ruby said, and she pulled him to her. She kissed him eagerly and Billy responded.

He showered quickly and brushed his teeth. He hung up his suit and returned to the bedroom in shirt and shorts. Ruby giggled.

'It's cold on the stairs,' Billy complained.

Ruby had found Radio Luxembourg and while the music wasn't all to Billy's taste, the disc jockey was playing some good popular records: The Platters' Smoke Gets in Your Eyes, Bobby Darin's Dream Lover and Buddy Holly's It Doesn't Matter Anymore. As Billy rounded the bed, the disc jockey played Johnny Ray singing Pink Sweater Angel. Must be an omen, thought Billy.

He sat on the edge of the bed and slipped off his shirt and shorts, folded them and laid them on the corner of Vic's bedside cabinet. He felt a little unsure now that the time had come, a little nervous. Would he achieve what he had set out to achieve? Would he let Ruby down? How high were her expectations? He tried not to hurry.

'Do you want the light left on?' he asked, as calmly as he could.

'Put the main light out,' Ruby said, 'and the

85

bedside lamp on.' Billy left the bed and pulled the light cord as Ruby switched on the small bedside lamp. 'Now this is really cosy' she said. 'Come here, Billy Walsh. I want this night to last forever.' She reached out for him and guided him onto the bed.

He lay alongside her and kissed her gently, his tongue probing slightly, his left hand cupping her breast as his thumb flicked over her nipple. He felt Ruby begin to breath hard. She placed her hand over his.

'Billy, wait,' she asked.

'What's wrong?' he asked, perplexed.

'Billy, I want you passionately, but I need you to be sure about me, so please listen to me for a moment.' Her voice shook a little as she told him of the other men in her life, of how they had used and abused her and how she had used them. She omitted nothing when she told him of her time with Stavros. Her voice was trembling and catching in her throat as she explained her greed in seeing in Stavros an easy road to riches, but realising her mistake too late. She told him how brutal Stavros could be, especially when it came to sex. They did it when, where and however he wanted it. There was no love in him, just rough, animal self-satisfaction.

'Enough,' Billy said and put a finger across her lips.

'Let me finish,' Ruby said. 'Since I've met you, Billy, you've treated me like a lady and yet you can't offer me the lifestyle Stavros can. For all that, I have fallen in love with you and if, after what you have heard, you still want me, I shall love you forever.'

Billy noticed a tear running down her cheek and kissed it away.

'Oh Ruby,' he sighed, 'I think I loved you from the moment I saw you. You didn't have to tell me about your past. Our future is more important, but you must know that my work in the merchant navy means I've had my share of flings, though that's all they were. No other woman has affected me like you. Maybe we could get somewhere to stay until the fuss dies down. Surely when he realises he can't get you back, Stavros will give you up. All I want is to make you happy for the rest of your life. I love you, Ruby.'

She stroked his hair. She was crying gently.

Billy could feel the wet tears as she whispered in his ear. 'Make love to me, Billy. Make me your woman.'

They kissed with passion. Their tongues met and he suddenly felt inflamed. He was now completely aroused. He kissed her neck, such a shapely neck, and then her shoulder. Her head went back, her red hair cascaded over the pillow, her back was arched and her breasts stood proud.

Billy caressed them and let his mouth float over them. Her nipples were now hard and tingling. He flicked his tongue over them and Ruby murmured a low contented moan of approval. Billy pinched at each nipple with his teeth and she squirmed in delight. With his tongue he now traced a line between her breasts, down to her stomach. Ruby's stomach muscles tightened involuntarily as Billy continued down. He tickled her pubic hair with his fingers and moved to kiss her hips.

Ruby turned slightly as Billy knelt on the bed.

He picked up her left leg by her ankle and kissed her calf and the outside of her thigh. She looked as he opened her legs.

She could see he was erect and firm. She wanted to touch him, but he would not let her, keeping just out of reach.

He then slowly kissed the inside of her thighs.

She groaned as she felt his hot breath on her most secret of places.

'Billy, please, you don't have to . . . '

She barely got the words out as he kissed her there. He didn't hear her words. This was Billy paying homage to the woman he loved.

The tip of his tongue touched her sensitive bud. It was like an electric shock. She cried with delight. Her body arched and as she opened her eyes, he was leaning over her, his hands either side of her shoulders.

She smiled as she said, 'Billy, that was wonderful. No one has ever treated me so gently and made me feel so good.' She reached out an elegant hand and found his penis. It was firm and hard. Her other hand squeezed him, almost hurting him as she fondled him with one hand and flicked the top of his penis with the other at the same time.

She offered her head up and he kissed her. She then took her mouth to his right shoulder and bit him. He sucked in air through clenched teeth, loving every second of it. She now guided him into her. He had to be careful, the sensation was enough to make him lose control and he wanted this to last as long as possible. He eased into her and let himself slowly lie on her. His head was on her breasts. This was heaven he thought.

Her legs were wide apart, her knees bent, as he raised himself. They moved slowly in unison, Ruby breathing in small quick breaths, Billy holding as long as possible. The rhythm picked up, Ruby was now rolling her head, suddenly she shouted.

'Now Billy, now. Please - please, now!' Billy felt himself explode, he shuddered from head to toe. It felt like his life blood had drained from him. Then a second wave, smaller, then a third, smaller still, then a tremor. He was finished.

Ruby had dug her nails into his buttocks. She was still rolling her head and vibrating softly as Billy withdrew from her. It was only then he noticed he was sweating and it had run into his eyes and stung him.

Ruby opened her eyes.

'Billy Walsh,' she purred, 'where have you been all my life? I never knew sex could be so good.'

'Still want to stay with me?' he asked.

'Oh, I won't be leaving you Billy, not ever.' Ruby lay back exhausted. 'But I want some more of that, before this night is out.' Billy reached for his cigarettes. He had a smile of satisfaction on his face.

Vic noticed the tall, heavy man walk away from Ada Molloy's gate.

'Look after the ale, Vinnie. I'll be back in a sec.' Vic quickly went out of the gate and made his way to the corner of Maidford Road. As he did so, he saw Alex getting into the Hillman.

The car started and moved towards Vic. Vic stepped back from the corner and lit a cigarette. As the car reached him it passed under a street lamp and Vic clearly saw the large blonde haired Alex and the more slightly built, Mediterranean looking Nikis.

Vic whistled slowly to himself. He noted the car: a Hillman Husky, registration 'ERG 766', dark colour, black or blue he thought. He walked back to the Walsh household. 'ERG 766' he kept repeating to himself. As he passed the Molloy's gate, he saw the curtains twitch and Ada Molloy peered out. Vic saluted her and she angrily closed the curtains. Vic knew something was wrong, but he figured Billy and Ruby were safe in his flat as no one else knew they were there. Let's get on with the do, he thought.

The Walshes' front door was open. Vic walked in to be greeted by the girls dancing to Lloyd Price singing Stagger Lee. The furniture had been pushed back to the walls, leaving plenty of floor space. Bobby and Dave were in one corner with a plate of sandwiches, spare ribs and a bottle of pale ale each. Kate, slightly tipsy, had mellowed and allowed the boys to take charge of the record player. After all, she wanted to dance and not be bothered changing records.

The three girls, Kate, Marie, and Sylvia, took turns in dancing with Tommy, Joe and Vic.

'Put Elvis on,' shouted Kate, as Stagger Lee finished. Bobby obliged and Teddy Bear, followed by I Got Stung, kept the girls dancing. Jack had knocked next door at the Shelton's and invited them in.

'Might as well join us,' he said. 'It looks like we'll keep you awake anyway.'

Jimmy Shelton was a big, dark man, with a hooked nose. His wife, Angela, was small and what he liked to call cuddly. They were good neighbours. Jimmy Shelton went into the kitchen and joined Vinnie Tillotson and Vic Scott, who had managed to escape the dancing attentions of the girls. Vinnie did the introductions.

'Watcha,' said Vic, as he proffered his hand,

'How do?' Jimmy said, as he poured a brown ale. 'I don't see Billy around.'

'He's taken his young lady home,' said Vic. 'He might join us later. Depends on how his luck is, I suppose.'

'If I know him, his luck will be good,' Jimmy said. 'The last do we had here was eighteen months ago. It was a lovely warm summers night and about midnight the music had quietened. We were mostly just talking. All of a sudden there was pandemonium from the chicken coop.

I came running out to see what the racket was and there was Billy with some blonde. She was stretched out on the coop and Billy was standing with his trousers round his ankles, performing good style. She was screaming, 'More Billy! More!' The hens were going berserk. The cockerel was looking on enviously, and I had to keep the kitchen door shut to stop any of the girls, or Mrs Walsh, coming out to see what was going on. Billy Walsh doesn't need any luck. He makes his own.'

Vinnie and Vic were laughing when Marie came into the kitchen, took Vic by the arm and dragged him into the front room.

'Come on, Vic,' she shouted, 'this is a nice slow one for you.' Elvis was singing A Fool Such As I.

Gordon and Vera Brown, from the house opposite, had come in. They were talking to Jack and Queenie. They too had noticed Billy was missing.

'Oh, he'll be here later,' said Mrs Walsh. 'He's taking a young lady home.'

Gordon winked at Vera. 'Hope he brings the Sunday papers in with him,' he said.

'Are we having a sing song, then?' Vera asked.

'As soon as these girls get tired, which shouldn't be too long now,' Jack replied, 'Tommy and Joe have got their guitars.'

'Oh, great,' said Vera. She loved a sing song. She was a big chested woman and fancied herself singing opera.

'Vinnie Tillotson! Get in here for a sing song!'

she shouted. Monica Tillotson popped her head round the kitchen door.

'Hello, Vera,' she said. 'Taken over already have you?' she laughed.

'Too right,' said Vera. 'Organisation is what's needed. Send that husband of yours in here.'

'You tell 'em, Vera girl,' shouted Tommy, as he reached for his guitar. The record finished and the girls flopped into the nearest available chair. Tommy and Joe began to tune up. 'What would you like?' asked Tommy.

'How about, Hey, Good Lookin'?' suggested Vera.

Vic intervened. 'Just before you start, did you hear about the sailor in Lime Street? He approached one of the ladies of the night and asked her, "How much?" "Two pounds," she said, "That's too expensive," he replied and approached another lady. "How much?" he asked and received the same reply. So he asked a third lady and she said, "One pound." "That sounds OK" he said, "but how come you're only charging half the price of the other girls?" "Because I have no womb," was her reply. "So what's that got to do with it?" asked the sailor. "Well," said the girl, "it means we'll have to do it against the wailings".'

The men laughed, the women giggled. Queenie Walsh tut-tutted.

They settled down and Tommy strummed Hey, Good Lookin' and Joe picked out a nice lead. Vinnie and Vera sang a duet and the rest of the company clapped their hands in time. They went from Hey, Good Lookin' to Who's Sorry Now? and He's Got the Whole World in His Hands, with Tommy and Joe swapping rhythm and lead.

Vic came up with an old cockney type song:

'I first met Nellie Hawkins dahn the Ould Kent Road.
Her hair was all dishevelled, she'd bin aht wiv Jimmy Brode.
She was a naughty ould gal,
Now she wore no blowses, an' I wore no trawsers
And she wore no under clothes
And when she caressed me, she almost molested me,
Such a feelin' no one knaws.
I said I'd like to love her, and don't treat me like a bruvver,
She said, I'll show you what you want to knows.
Now the Doctor says, wiv a twinkle, the eye of your winklle
Is just like a big red rose.'

The girls were blushing, the men were cheering.

'Vic, that's rude,' Mrs Walsh complained, which had the men laughing all the more.

'Course it's rude, mother,' Jack bawled. 'It's a cockney sea song. It's bound to be rude.'

More drink was passed around and Tommy played The Story of My Life and Tom Dooley.

Jack Walsh was standing in the kitchen, eating a sandwich when Queenie found him,

'Our Billy's late.' She sounded sad.

'Didn't expect him myself, 'Jack replied. He turned and put his hands on Queenie's shoulders. 'Ruby is a very attractive girl. Billy is in love with her. Who wouldn't want to be in our Billy's shoes? You'll have to get used to the idea of seeing more of Ruby. I think this is the girl Billy has been looking for.'

'It's not that I don't like her, Jack, I hardly know her. But I have this feeling. She is trouble.'

'Well, she's not trouble tonight, so let's get back in the front room and enjoy ourselves.'

The guests were sat in a circle on the living room floor, swaying side to side, while Tommy and Joe played All I Have To Do Is Dream.

Jack noticed Vic and Marie were sat together, and Marie had linked Vic's arm. Although there was some eight years age difference, they looked like they would make a good couple. Jack thought she could do worse than Vic.

Bobby and Dave had curled up in the armchairs and dropped off to sleep.

'Too much light ale,' said Queenie.

Jack agreed. They sat on the couch and joined in the singing.

'Well, mother,' Jack said, 'looks like we are in for a long night. I only wish our Billy was here. He's missing all the fun.'

'Somehow I don't think he's missing any fun at all,' Queenie Walsh replied.

17

The blonde's name was Paula. Stavros had asked her name when he had finished with her. He handed her another twenty pounds.

'Paula, you have been a good girl.' he said.

Paula could hardly reply. Her lips were swollen, her ribs ached from his great weight. Her arms were bruised from his heavy hands and her eyes were red and stinging. He had, to all intents and purposes, raped her twice and once forced her to perform oral sex. He had not been slow to slap her when she had not responded quickly enough to his demands. She stuffed her underclothes and nylons into her coat pocket as he let her out of the room.

'Next time I'm in London, I'll ask Kris to get you for me,' he said, matter-of-factly. He closed the door and she made her way down the stairs.

She walked with difficulty, her whole body aching inside and out. She had to wake the night porter to open the main door. He gave her just a cursory glance, another one on the game, he thought, as she stepped out into the cold night.

There was an icy wind and a frost on the pavements, and as the porter closed the door, he heard the girl let out a scream of pain and despair. The porter returned to his desk as his phone rang.

'Mr Ziacos here, room twenty-seven. Any coffee available?'

'I'll have to check in the kitchens, sir.'

'Well, check and if you come up with coffee and say a couple of cheese sandwiches, I'll make it worth your while.'

'Oh, I'll sort something out for you, sir,' the porter was quick to respond. Fifteen minutes later, he was knocking on the door of room twenty-seven.

Stavros opened the door. He had just a towel wrapped around his ample waist and his large stomach hung over the towel. He was still wet, having just stepped out of the shower.

The porter was shocked at his size, not because he was fat, but his shoulders were huge, as were his biceps and forearms. Wouldn't like to fight my way out of a tight corner with him, he thought

'One cheese, one corned beef sandwich and a pot of coffee OK, sir?' he said politely.

'Good man,' Stavros said, and he indicated that the tray could be left on the bedside table. He gave the porter two pound notes.

'What time do you go off duty?'

'Eight o'clock sir.'

'Good, I'm going to enjoy the coffee and have a nap, but I'm expecting a long distance call from Liverpool in the next couple of hours, so don't hesitate to wake me. Do you understand?'

'Yes sir, you can rely on me,' said the porter.

'Good man,' Stavros said again. 'There will, of course, be something more in it for you. By the way, you didn't see a blonde leaving here at any time tonight, did you?'

'Me? I never saw anyone or anything all night,' said the porter.

'Good man, good man,' Stavros praised him, as he ushered him out of the room. He closed and locked the door and returned to the bed. He ate greedily and drank his coffee noisily. He lit a cigar and inhaled deeply. Feeling refreshed, he stretched out on the bed and began to nod off. As he did so, he thought if the boys ring me later with a good result in Liverpool, it won't have been a bad night after all. That Paula was a good thing, even though I had to be a bit persuasive once or twice. Soon he was asleep and had started to snore.

Alex woke with a start, the alarm clock which he had found in the spare bedroom, rang loudly. He accidentally kicked it over, then wearily hoisted himself out of the armchair, picked up the clock and turned off the alarm.

'Four o'clock! Jesus Christ!' he muttered. 'Four o'clock. Four hours sleep. Four o'clock!'

Nikis had claimed the settee, so Alex kicked his feet off the arm.

'What the bleedin' hell's going on?' Nikis moaned.

'It's four o'clock,' Alex said. 'I'm going for a piss, then I'll make some coffee. We'll have to make a move.'

'OK, I'm ready when you are,' Nikis replied. He sat up and rubbed the sleep out of his eyes, 'Four o'clock? Are we fucking crazy or what?'

Alex came back carrying two cups of steaming hot coffee. 'Well, at least we managed to get warm and have some kip.'

'Yeah, four hours is better than nothing,' Nikis said.

Alex asked Nikis if he had all he required for the job.

Nikis checked. 'Crowbar, tape, four pound lump hammer, knife, knuckle-duster. Yeah, I'm kitted out with all I need,' he said in a chilling tone.

Alex was satisfied. 'Right, we agree on the strategy,' he said, 'so let's go through it again. I don't want any slip-ups. We park on the car sales lot facing in the direction of Old Swan. I jemmy the door. Should be easy enough. You race up the stairs and take the knife to 'Fred Astair'. He won't argue with that. I follow you and grab Ruby. You put him out of action and I tape Ruby's hands and feet. Once he's dealt with, we carry her down to the entry. You go for the car, stop at the gate, open the tailgate and in she goes.'

'A piece of piss,' Nikis smiled.

'So what's the lump hammer for?' Alex asked.

'Just to stop the dancer from trying to follow us,' Nikis said. He smiled again, a crazy smile.

'It's four-twenty,' Alex noted. 'Let's move. I think by half-five we can ring Stavros with some good news.'

18

Knotty Ash, Liverpool
4.30am

Ruby stirred. For a moment she panicked, then realised she was with Billy. The panic turned to excitement as she reached for him. Her hand stroked his chest and he slowly opened his eyes.

'God, I needed that sleep,' he said as he smiled.

Ruby leaned over him and kissed him.

He reached for her, but she pushed him back.

'What time is it?' he asked.

'It's half-four and it's my turn to do the work,' she replied. Ruby felt Billy was already aroused. She stroked him gently and she bit his nipples. He moaned in ecstasy. Ruby straddled him and let her firm breasts fall onto his face. She pulled his head into them and they swayed gently. She took the pillows and put them behind him. Moving back on her knees, she could feel his firmness. She took it and slowly sank over it. They were perfectly coupled, face to face.

They kissed a fiercely, open mouthed and wet. She raised and lowered herself on Billy. He could not believe such pleasure was possible. They broke for breath. He caressed her nipples, while she ran her hands through his hair.

'Oh, Billy,' she whispered, 'this is wonderful. Tell me when you are ready. I want to enjoy this with you.' She leaned back, her hands on the bed, as she moved up and down.

He could see the whole magnificent sight. He wanted it to last forever, but he knew it could not. He sucked in air and she knew this was it, she increased the tempo and now she was bleating with delight as she felt the great crescendo turn into the miracle of the climax. Then as she cried out in delirious delight, the bedroom door burst open and in ran Nikis and Alex.

Queenie Walsh sat bolt upright in bed. She did not know what had woken her. She switched on the bedside lamp and glanced at the clock: a quarter-to-five. She looked at Jack. He was sound asleep. Too many pints of mild, she thought. She got out of bed and went downstairs. She took in the sight of her living room: bodies everywhere, empty beer bottles, half full glasses and half eaten sandwiches. What a mess, she thought. Still, a cup of tea for now, then back to bed. She'd think about cleaning up later, much later. She walked into the kitchen and there was Tommy pouring boiling water into the teapot.

'Tea, Ma?' he said.

'What are you doing up?' she asked.

'Can't be sure. Something woke me a few minutes ago and I couldn't get back to sleep So I decided to make a cuppa.'

'Is our Billy home?' asked Queenie.

'No, he's not. And do you know, as I woke I felt frightened for him. I think that's why I couldn't sleep. Do you think he's all right with Ruby, Ma?'

'I don't know, son, but I know what you mean about a strange feeling,' Queenie Walsh replied with more than a hint of fear in her voice.

19

4.45am

Ada Molloy was on her fourth pot of tea since midnight. She knew it was useless to go to bed, so she elected to use the couch, where she slept fitfully. She now sat drinking tea and opening a second packet of twenty cigarettes, still brooding, still unhappy and still convinced that Billy Walsh was the cause of all their troubles.

Michael and Agnes had gone to their beds, leaving her with her thoughts, which had fermented and boiled up to a black morass inside her head. On each occasion she had woken during the night, she had gone to her front door and seen the lights still on in the Walsh household. She had heard the sounds of laughter and music, and this had compounded her hatred. She also wanted to know if the information which Michael had given to Alex had resulted in spoiling Billy Walsh's night of passion.

She finished a second cup of tea and lit another cigarette. The need to know was now getting the better of her. She knew she would have to go to the Walsh's house and ask if Billy was home yet. She needed to hear that he had to drop everything, including his new fancy bit, and report back to his ship. She needed to laugh at the Walsh family and tell them that she gave away his whereabouts. She was craving for this satisfaction as she slipped on her shoes and a cardigan, and made the short walk to the Walsh's, two houses away.

Police Constable Drummond sipped at his hot mug of tea. He felt the warm liquid through his chest and he wrapped his hands around the mug, warming his fingers. He had been to Broadgreen Hospital to get details of Francis' injuries from the doctor who treated him, then he had to visit a newspaper kiosk, reported by a publicly spirited passer-by as having been broken into. The lock on the kiosk door had been jemmied and it looked like sweets and cigarettes had been stolen.

A five minute ride on his Vespa motorscooter had taken him to the owners home. Then he had to return and wait for him to arrive and secure the kiosk. By then the cold had caught up with him. He was pleased to be back in the station.

'Two and a quarter hours to go,' he said to his sergeant. 'Should be quiet now it's Sunday morning.' Bulldog stretched his legs out in front of the small electric fire. 'It's a funny do, that Francis Molloy beating, Sarge.'

'How do you mean?' the sergeant asked.

'Well, a complete stranger apparently buys him a couple of drinks, asks about Billy Walsh and the redhead with him, then beats the shit out of Francis in the Gents. Now I know Francis is a bit lukewarm, but he didn't deserve that. I reckon Billy or Tommy Walsh are involved in this even though they don't know it. That Billy Walsh is always playing around with someone's woman. I'll be speaking to him on Monday.'

'If it's quiet, I'll get Jock to speak to him later today,' the sergeant replied.

'Thanks, Sarge.' Bulldog glanced up at the wall-clock. 'It's five o'clock. Fancy another brew before I check around the patch.' P.C. Drummond filled the kettle and placed it on the solitary gas ring.

He was looking forward to going home for a long sleep in a warm bed, when the telephone rang.

20

Piccadilly, London
5.30am

Stavros Ziacos slept well, even though he had Ruby on his mind. Could it be put down to the fact that in the last eighteen hours or so, he had eaten well, drunk copiously and had sex in one form or another, six times. He had intended just napping and lying on top of his bed, but his exertions had caught up with him and he was now fast asleep, his huge frame rising and falling evenly, as he breathed slowly.

He did not hear his phone ring, nor hear his door open or the night porter make his way across the room. The porter stood nervously over Stavros, undecided where to touch him. Eventually, he poked a finger into his shoulder.

'Mr Ziacos! Mr Ziacos! Your phone-call from Liverpool.'

Stavros grunted, still half asleep. He pushed the porter's arm away.

The porter poked him again.

This time Stavros woke fully and seized the porter by his shirt, throwing him over the bed.

'What the fuck are you up to?' he growled.

'Mr Ziacos, your phone-call!' the porter stammered. 'You said it was important and you did not answer your telephone, so I thought I had better wake you.'

'Oh, good man, good man,' Stavros said. He took a pound note from his bedside cabinet and gave it to the porter. 'What time is it?' he asked.

'Five-thirty. The caller from Liverpool is holding,' the porter replied.

'I'll take the call here,' Stavros indicated. 'Go and switch it through and remember, no listening, or I will be very angry.'

'You can count on me, sir,' said the porter, as he backed hastily out of the room.

Ada Molloy knocked on the door of number twenty-two. She was shivering with cold. The wind had strengthened, and although she had only walked twenty yards or so, she felt the icy wind piercing her.

Tommy Walsh opened the door.

'Oh, it's you Ada. What are you after?'

'Is Queenie still up?' Ada asked, through chattering teeth.

'You'd better come in,' Tommy said. 'We've just made a pot of tea. Or would you prefer something stronger?'

'A scotch would be nice,' Ada replied, as she picked her way through the sleeping bodies in the living room and into the kitchen where Queenie had been joined by her husband. 'I've had enough tea for one night.'

'Well, Ada, to what do we owe the pleasure?' asked Queenie.

'I couldn't sleep,' Ada said, 'and I remembered

I had a message for Billy from the shipping company.'

'What message?' asked Jack. 'Our Billy's home for five days yet. There's been no one here from the shipping company.'

'So Billy isn't home then?' Ada sounded surprised and she went on to describe the conversation with the stranger who said he was from the shipping company.

'Michael told him where Vic lived?' Tommy said with alarm. 'I'll have to wake Vic up.'

Queenie Walsh was trembling.

'Jack, I told you,' she said. 'That Ruby one is trouble.'

'You don't know that yet, Mother,' was all Jack would say.

Ada Molloy's initial satisfaction was now turning to concern. She was beginning to realise she may have caused more trouble than she had intended, when Vic, having heard the story repeated for his benefit, called her a stupid hate-filled bitch.

21

5.05am

Bulldog Drummond was heading into the wind on his Vespa as he passed the Knotty Ash Hotel. Could be snow by daylight, he thought, as he pulled over in front of the barber's. An ambulance was already there and a number of people were standing in the small entry.

'Do you all live here?' Bulldog asked. They nodded. 'Then if you heard or saw anything, give me your flat number and we'll get to you as soon as we can. Who rang 999?'

'I did,' said the newsagent. The constable went with him to his flat and used his phone. He spoke with his sergeant and arranged for someone from Derby Lane station to come and assist in taking statements. He also asked for CID once he realised it was Billy Walsh and the second serious beating he had attended in eight hours, just one hundred yards apart.

Billy Walsh was in a bad way. The ambulance men were making him secure on a stretcher and they told Bulldog he could not walk. They feared his ankles were broken, along with broken ribs and cheek bone.

The newsagent said he heard a woman screaming and thought he saw someone being bundled into a car, undressed except for a fur coat. It looked like her ankles were bound with tape and the car, possibly a black Hillman, sped off towards Old Swan.

The ambulance left for Broadgreen Hospital.

Bulldog told the driver someone would visit Billy later. A car pulled up and a CID and a uniformed officer from the Derby Lane station got out. Bulldog spoke to the CID man. He gave the other officer the flat numbers of potential witnesses and asked him to collect their statements.

The CID man stayed at the scene as Bulldog drove off along East Prescot Road, the small windshield affording him little protection against a bitter wind. He turned left into Kings Avenue and stopped outside number twenty-two. He walked up the path and knocked on the door just as Ada swallowed her second whisky and tried once again to express some regret for what she had done.

Queenie Walsh opened the door.

'Mrs Walsh,' Bulldog said, 'there's been some trouble.'

He said no more before Queenie fainted.

Ruby lay on the couch, staring at Alex. She could not speak because of the tape across her mouth. Alex had at least fastened a couple of buttons on her coat, though he had done it very slowly, and not before he had let Nikis have a good look and a fondle of her breasts.

'Very nice,' Nikis kept repeating.

'Stavros will kill you for this,' she spat.

'We think not,' Nikis said, as he ran his hands between her thighs. 'Very nice, I think before this day is over you will be nice to me,' he threatened.

'Tape her mouth while I call Stavros,' Alex ordered.

Ruby watched in fear as Alex asked the operator to put him through to the Hamilton Hotel, Piccadilly, London.

'Hello, Boss, we have some good news for you. Yeah, she's here. We had to be a little rough, though. She wasn't exactly happy to come with us.'

Stavros asked about Billy and Alex told him how they had taken him by surprise. He didn't describe the position Billy and Ruby were in, but he told him how Billy had thrown himself in front of Ruby and how, as Nikis moved in, he had tried to butt him. 'Nikis is some mover in a scrap, Boss. Quick as a cobra. He dodged the butt and punched Billy three times in the ribcage. Knocked the wind right out of him. Then with his knuckle-duster, he caught him a lovely right hook on his left cheek and split it open. Must be broken, Boss.' Alex continued as Stavros enjoyed the detail. 'That put the guy out of the game. Ruby by this time was screaming, so we had to slap her. Only fair, Boss. We didn't want the neighbours to come looking. Anyway, we were about to leave, when Nikis goes to the door and comes back with his lump hammer and calm as you like, gives each of this fellas' ankles a good smack. "That will stop him dancing for a while,' says Nikis and off we scampered with Ruby.'

Stavros was a happy man and told Alex so. 'Keep Ruby there until I get back. I hope to be home for tonight.'

Ruby, gagged and bound, lived through the whole horrific episode again as Alex related it to Stavros. She could do nothing, but lie there with her head was swimming. She passed out.

22

5.45am

Jack Walsh had reached the top of the stairs as Queenie collapsed. He hurried down and helped Bulldog carry her into the kitchen. They made her comfortable and quickly revived her. Tommy made a fresh pot of tea as the officer related what had happened to Billy.

'There must be a link with what happened to your Francis,' he directed the remark at Ada. She told Bulldog that Francis had said his assailant had asked about Billy and Ruby.

'I knew there was a connection,' Bulldog said. 'It must be something to do with Billy and his fondness for married women. It wouldn't be the first time, now would it?'

'OK' Jack said. 'You may be right, but these are two serious assaults. I suggest you make some headway in finding who's responsible before we do. Otherwise there'll be more trouble than you can handle.'

Tommy, who had tried to keep himself under control, now exploded.

'This fancy bastard has made a big mistake and I'm going to get him. I don't care what I have to do, but I'll get even for our Billy!'

'Now, son, take it easy,' Bulldog said. That sort of talk could get you locked up.'

'Don't even think about stopping me! You can lock me up when it's all over, but not before I've finished.'

Bulldog drank his tea and left his station number with Jack saying he would be grateful for any information.

'Let the police deal with it,' he said, as he made his way down the path to his motor scooter.

The neighbours had gone home, but Bobby, Dave and the girls were still asleep in the front room. Just as well, thought Queenie, as she closed the kitchen door so as not to wake them.

They sat around the kitchen table: Queenie, Jack, Tommy, Joe, Vic and Ada Molloy.

'So what do we do?' asked Tommy.

'We get the bastard,' Jack spat it out. 'No one does this to my family.'

'Let's pool our information,' said Tommy. 'Vic, tell me what you know. And how are we fixed for the use of a car?'

Vic told them about the Hillman and gave them it's registration number. 'There were two of them,' he said, before going on to tell them what he knew about Stavros and that he lived somewhere in Old Swan.

'I don't have a road name, but it's not far from Derby Lane.'

'If our Billy is able to talk when we get to the hospital,' Jack said, 'he should be able to give us a road name.'

Queenie Walsh shuddered. 'Be careful. You're

not on the docks now! These men are professionals.'

'Professionals or not,' Jack snapped back, 'they've only dealt with Francis and Billy, neither of whom you would describe as hard cases.

'I'll be ready for them!' Tommy said, pounding the kitchen table.

'I'm with you on this one,' Joe cut in, 'but don't tell the girls until it's all over.'

Vic said he would go to his flat and make good the damage.

'Ring me from the hospital when you're on your way and I'll have a car ready for you. Tell Billy I'll be in to see him later.'

Jack stood up. 'I'm going to get ready to visit Billy. Someone will have to go to the phone and call a cab. It's too cold and wet to walk that far.'

Ada said she would go to the phone. 'As long as I can come with you,' she added. 'I'll talk to Francis and see if he knows any more than he's telling the police.'

Queenie fetched everyone's coats and urged them to leave by the back door. 'Don't wake the young ones,' she said. 'The less they know the better at this stage.'

Fifteen minutes later the cab arrived. It was a short, but silent journey to Broadgreen Hospital. The light, overnight snow had turned to a heavy sleet as the first glimmer of light showed in the eastern sky. It was seven o'clock as the taxi rolled into the hospital grounds.

The five of them reached the ward without

being challenged. There they came across Ward Sister Pringle.

'William Walsh is in theatre,' she said, 'having his ankles encased in plaster. He is not likely to be back on the ward for at least another hour and then he'll be allowed just two visitors at a time.' She spat this out in a machine-gun chatter, hands on hips, feet planted firmly apart in a 'this is my domain' body gesture.

'My arse!' snorted Jack Walsh, 'We're waiting right here and as soon as my lad comes back, he'll see as many people as he damn well pleases.'

23

Picadiily, London
10am

Stavros woke and checked his watch Ten o'clock. For a moment he thought he was late, then he realised it was Sunday and he was not expected at the Olympia Restaurant until two. He decided on a leisurely breakfast and perhaps a bottle of wine at noon, just to celebrate the fact that Alex and Nikis had resolved his little problem in Liverpool.

He rang for room service and talked them into bringing him a breakfast with the Sunday papers. He showered, dressed and lit a cigar. He sat enjoying his smoke while waiting for the food and his thoughts turned to the matter of what to do with Ruby. She would, of course, have to go. He could not keep her, not now some two-bit merchant seaman had screwed her. He would lose face and the respect of his men if he kept her. He would have to let her go, but not before he had seen to it that no other man would ever be attracted to her again.

Alex had locked Ruby in the spare room. He had allowed her a dressing gown and a pair of slippers and had left her sandwiches and coffee.

'Don't even think about asking for anything for the next four hours,' he said. 'Nikis and I are going to catch up on our kip.' He leered at her.

'That is,' he said, 'unless you want me to give you a real seeing to. Much better than the sailor.'

Ruby spat at him and Nikis leaped at her, snatching her head back by her hair. He slapped her twice.

'Soon you will beg for me,' he whispered and put his lips to hers, hard and crushing, until she tasted her own blood. At the same time, he cupped her breast and pinched her nipple until she pulled away, screaming.

He left the room and she heard the key turn in the lock. She sat on the bed, and began to cry, but not for long. She had to keep as calm as possible. She knew there had to be a way out of this and she knew she had to get to Billy before Stavros came home.

She poured herself a cup of coffee and sitting on the bed decided she could use Nikis to escape. She lay back and allowed herself to sleep a little. She would need all her strength to deal with Nikis.

She had been asleep for only a couple of hours when she was woken by the telephone ringing. She heard Alex's voice.

'Yeah, Boss, everything is OK. No, the police never saw us. Yeah, she's in the spare room. She's not going anywhere, Boss. She's only wearing her dressing gown and slippers. Don't worry, Boss. Everything's under control. OK, Boss. Seven o'clock at Lime Street Station. By the taxi rank on Skelhorne Street. Yeah, I know it. I'll be there.'

So he's coming home tonight, Ruby thought. She panicked a little. She would definitely have to get away and soon. Stavros would be much harder on her than Nikis or Alex.

24

Noon

Queenie and Jack were about to leave Billy and let him get some sleep. It was some three hours since he had come back from theatre, and while he had been willing to talk to them about what had happened, it had taken its toll.

Tommy and Joe had earlier made their way to Vic's to pick up a car and Ada Molloy had spoken to Francis. On hearing the description of Billy's assailant, he confirmed it was the same person.

Queenie Walsh looked around the ward as they were leaving. It was sparsely furnished, with white walls and a green floor covering. It was a Spartan place and she hoped she would not have to come back to visit Tommy.

Sister Pringle reminded them that visiting was from six until seven. Not a moment earlier or later.

'Bollocks!' was all Jack Walsh would say as they left the ward.

They waited at the bus stop.

'I hope Tommy and Joe get a result,' Jack said.

Ada Molloy was still showing remorse. 'I don't want any more trouble,' she said, 'but I would like to see this bastard taken care of . I just wish I had someone who could help.'

'You can help, Ada,' Queenie said, 'by keeping

your own counsel in future. You know none of my boys would hurt Francis. They grew up with him. You let your envy get the better of you and you had to blame someone. So you picked on Billy, because you thought he insulted you.'

'I know I'm wrong,' said Ada, 'but I didn't think it would come to this. You're a lucky woman, Queenie Walsh. You've got three good sons and a doting daughter and look what I've ended up with. A Nancy boy, a sneak thief and a daughter with looks like a blunt axe and a brain no sharper.' She snivelled into her handkerchief, as Queenie patted her arm.

'Here's the bus,' Jack said, and as they found a seat, he insisted Ada came home with them for a cup of tea. 'You can sit with us until Tommy and Joe get back.'

This suggestion cheered Ada a little and she resolved that perhaps the Walshes weren't such bad neighbours after all.

25

1.30pm

Vic had driven the length of Prescot Road, east and west, for the fourth time.

Joe said, 'Let's pull in to the Cygnet pub. It's half an hour to closing time. We can have a drink and ask a few questions.'

'Good idea,' Tommy replied.

They parked the car in Derby Lane and walked into the bar of the Cygnet Hotel.

'Three halves of bitter,' Vic said.

When the barman had finished serving them, Vic asked him if he was working the previous night. The barman confirmed he was and Vic described Ruby and Billy to him. 'Did you see them at all?' he asked.

'Do I recall them?' the barman exclaimed. 'I'll say. He was stood at the bar. Very sharp dresser. Drank Highballs. She came in ten minutes later. What a looker! What an entrance! The customers couldn't believe their eyes and there were one or two whistles. They didn't stay long. Only had the one drink.'

Vic ordered another three halves and he gave the barman a good tip.

'I think we are in the right area,' he said to Tommy and Joe. 'Let's leave the car and have a walk around.'

'Good idea,' Tommy replied. 'It's dried up now and not so windy.'

They left the pub and stood on the corner of Derby Lane and Prescot Road.

Joe said, 'She has to live within walking distance of the pub. She wouldn't have travelled any great distance to meet Billy here. Billy would have done the travelling.'

'I think you're right,' Tommy agreed. 'Assuming she's as wealthy as she appears, she's not going to live in one of those small terraced houses over the road. She's more likely to live on Derby Lane or off Prescot Road, along Greenfield Road. Let's take a walk. If we keep turning left we should complete a square and end up back here.'

'Right, let's go,' said Vic. 'The weather might have dried up, but it's still too cold to hang about.'

They set off along Derby Lane, past the police station and Billy Martin's Dance School. They had walked about half-a-mile in the direction of Queen's Drive and were approaching the Conservative Club.

'Take a left here into Brookland Road East,' Vic said. 'There are some big houses with drives down here.' Half-way along Brookland Road East, on the left, was Greenfield Road. 'Up here now,' Vic said, 'This will take us back to the pub.'

'Isn't there a church and a jewellers on the corner?' said Joe.

'You're right,' Tommy replied, 'and there are some big posh houses here.'

They walked up Greenfield Road, looking up the driveways. As they reached the last house before the church they had resigned themselves to finding nothing when Vic noticed the black Hillman Husky.

'ERG 766!' he yelled, 'That's the car I saw last night! This must be the place.'

As they opened the gate, they heard a smashing of glass and a woman's voice screaming. They raced up the drive towards the house as the front door was flung open and all three recognised Ruby rushing out.

Alex and Nikis were right behind her.

26

2pm

Ruby banged on the bedroom door. She needed to use the toilet and she shouted to Nikis to let her out. Alex was asleep, so Nikis climbed the stairs wearily and unlocked the door.

'Make it quick!' he said.

'Give me a break,' Ruby replied, 'I've been in there for three and a half hours. I need to use the toilet and freshen up.'

Nikis followed her along the landing to the bathroom.

'Leave the door open!' he ordered.

'Pervert!' Ruby snapped.

Ruby used the toilet and kept her dressing gown wrapped around her. She could see Nikis glancing through the open door. Looking down, she saw a bottle of bleach at the side of the toilet pan. She reached down and slid it under her dressing gown. As she looked out, she could see Nikis lighting a cigarette. Standing up quickly, she stepped over to the wash basin.

'Get a move on,' Nikis said, tiredly.

Ruby did not reply. Instead, she let her dressing gown slip off her shoulders as she wet the back of her neck with the flannel.

Nikis saw his chance and, with Alex asleep, knew it was time to make his move. He stepped into the bathroom and reached for Ruby. His hand slipped around her and he reached for a breast.

Ruby moaned and Nikis relaxed. He put a hand on her shoulder to turn her, but as he did, she swung round with the bleach bottle in her right hand. The cap was missing and she threw the contents with all the force she could muster into Nikis' face. He was too relaxed to react quickly enough, and though he put his arm up to protect his eyes, he could not stop all the bleach finding its target. She then brought the bottle down on Nikis' head, pushed him away from her and made for the stairs.

Nikis was screaming and shouting for Alex, and as she reached the foot of the stairs, Alex came from the side room into the hallway, still wiping the sleep from his eyes. Ruby was the last person he expected to see and he was taken by surprise as she ran past him, making for the door.

Nikis was stumbling down the stairs. 'Stop the bitch!' he shouted. 'She tried to fuckin' blind me!'

Alex made a despairing dive for Ruby, but as she flung the door open, it slammed into Alex's head and shattered a glass panel. As she ran to the driveway screaming she saw Vic, Tommy and Joe coming through the front gate. She ran into Vic's arms.

'Oh, Vic! Help me, help me!' she shouted

'It's OK,' said Vic. 'You're safe now.'

Tommy knew who he wanted.

'Take care of him, Joe,' he said, pointing to

Alex. He was up to the front door as Nikis was ready to take him, but Tommy was too quick and Nikis, hindered by the bleach, was not as formidable as he might have been. Tommy head-butted him and opened up a gash above his eyes. He then stunned him with a couple of straight lefts and put his top teeth through his bottom lip with a vicious right uppercut.

Nikis fell back into the porch and made no attempt to get up.

'Get me to the hospital,' was all he could say, 'I've got bleach in my eyes.'

Tommy ignored him and went over to where Joe was holding Alex against the car.

'Let's have everyone in the house,' he said. 'Ruby, go and get dressed and call the police and an ambulance.'

'Where's your boss?' he asked Alex, but Alex was saying nothing. 'You'll have to talk to the police sooner or later,' Tommy said.

Ruby pulled Tommy to one side and she told him of the phone call she had overheard. Stavros, she said, was due back in Liverpool at seven.

'That's great,' said Tommy. 'We'll let the police have these two now and they can pick up your husband when he gets home tonight.'

Ruby took the keys to the Humber and told Tommy she was going to visit Billy.

'What about the police?' Tommy protested.

'Tell them I'll be back,' Ruby said, 'and you and Joe wait here for me.' With that she was gone.

Tommy heard the Humber start up and as it pulled out onto Prescot Road, a police car passed it, turning into Greenfield Road, followed by an ambulance.

27

2.30pm

From Greenfield Road to the traffic lights at the junction of Prescot Road, Derby Lane, and St. Oswald Street is about five hundred yards. The big Humber covered this distance in seconds and as it reached the junction, the lights were changing from green to amber. But Ruby was not about to stop. Fortunately, on a cold and wet Sunday afternoon in Liverpool, the amount of traffic on the road was minimal.

As the lights hit red, Ruby slammed the car into third gear and swung it right into St. Oswald Street. She forced the accelerator down and the two-and-a-half-litre engine roared as the car easily took the rising road in the melting snow. The rear of the vehicle slued towards the kerb.

Ruby, intent only on getting to the hospital before the police insisted on her making statements, wrestled with the steering wheel and righted the car.

'Slow down,' she said to herself out loud, 'or you'll end up in hospital yourself.'

She reached the top of St. Oswald Street, only to find the traffic lights were against her. She stopped and looking ahead and to her right, saw the roads deserted. She checked her mirrors and saw only a bus coming up behind her. She selected first gear and took off through the lights, making a left turn into Edge Lane.

Broadgreen Hospital was now about a mile away. It took Ruby ninety seconds to reach it. She left the car unlocked and half mounted on the kerb outside the main entrance. Panting, she ran into the foyer and past the enquiry desk before the attendant could ask her who she was looking for.

Tommy had shouted to her as she left the house, 'Ward D4.'

She quickly took in the information on the boards: D1, D2, and D3. Where's D4, she thought. Just my luck. One, two, and three, but no four. She looked again. It was in the opposite direction. The arrow pointing to the left indicated wards D4 and D5. She ran, breathless now, up two flights of stairs. At the top, she turned right. The ward was some twenty yards away at the end of the corridor.

Ruby stopped and composed herself. After a couple of deep breaths, she walked quickly to the ward. Sister Pringle bumped into Ruby as she turned into the corridor.

'What are you doing here?' she said pompously. ' There is no visiting until six o'clock!'

'I want to see Billy Walsh,' Ruby gasped out and tried to push past the sister, but the nurse would not budge.

'Visiting time is at six o'clock!' she said firmly. Ruby shoved her hard against the wall.

'I'm going to see my man. Don't try and stop me. I'm in enough trouble, so dealing with you won't make much difference. Now get out of my way!'

Sister Pringle stepped aside.

'You haven't heard the last of this,' she said, 'I'm going for the orderlies'.'

Ruby ignored her and walked into the ward. What she saw stopped her in her tracks.

28

Billy Walsh was beginning to feel a little better. It was now some four hours since he had returned from theatre and he had managed to sleep for a couple of hours since his family had left. Now, except for the pain in his ankles and his cracked rib, he was feeling less uncomfortable.

The major reason for his improvement, though, was nurse Linda Watson. Nurse Watson was a small bubbly blonde, with a nice bedside manner. She had kept an eye on Billy and he had kept an ever improving eye on her. It started with a smile, and a 'thank you,' when she poured him some Lucozade. Then Billy, forgetting his injuries and acting on instinct, asked her if she liked to dance.

'I like to dance, but I'm not too good,' she replied.

This was music to Billy's ears. 'I could teach you when I'm fit again.'

'Now you might be a long time getting fit enough to dance,' she chided, gently.

'Time to get to know you then,' Billy said.

Nurse Watson looked at him. She could see that behind the damaged face was a handsome man. Perhaps she would take him up on his offer. 'Nurses are not allowed to fraternise with the patients.' she said, instead.

'I won't be a patient forever,' Billy said, then he let out a groan as he moved and his ribs hurt. The nurse rushed to him.

'Are you hurting?' she asked, concern showing in her voice.

'I need to move, but I can't,' he said.

She reached over him to help, She put her hands under his arms and he put his hands on her shoulders. He eased himself up onto his pillows and, as he did, their faces all but met. Billy never missed an opportunity in his life, and let his swollen lips touch her cheek.

'You are the only medicine I need,' he whispered.

She smiled and stroked his cheek. It was then that, over her shoulder, Billy saw Ruby standing at the entrance to the ward.

He was about to shout her name, when he saw the look of disbelief on her face. He saw her hand go up to her mouth, then she turned and was gone. Billy tried to shout after her, but his words were not loud enough. The louder he spoke, the more his face hurt. He was reduced to whispering.

'Ruby, come back.'

Linda looked around, to see Ruby turn and run. 'Don't worry,' she said. 'I'll look after you. And, as you say, you won't always be a patient, will you?'

Billy sank back onto the pillows. I always fuck it up, he thought, and he lay there thinking about the pleasures he and Ruby had enjoyed. Then he remembered Nikis attacking him and his failed attempt to head butt him. Nikis, like an ABA champion, had taken him out with three blows. He grimaced as he recalled watching pathetically while Alex was slapping Ruby. Then came the final indignity of Nikis smashing his ankles. And here I am, he thought, chatting up the nurse with Ruby watching.

A tear ran down his cheek and as his body shook, the stabbing pains returned to his ribs and he cried out. Nurse Watson ran to him and wiped his eyes.

'Where are you hurting, Billy?' she asked.

'I'm hurting inside,' he replied.

29

Crewe Station, Cheshire
6pm

Stavros Ziacos lit a cigar while he watched the British Rail bar steward pour him a couple of miniature whiskeys into a glass. He was feeling pleased. The afternoon business in London had gone well. The solicitors had rubber-stamped the deal and soon he was going to be a rich man.

The train pulled out of Crewe Station and within an hour he would be back in Liverpool. He paid for his drink and topped up the glass with Canada Dry. He took a large pull on the glass, felt the warmth of the liquid on the back of his throat and it felt good. He felt good. He was going to feel even better once he had dealt with Ruby.

There were plenty more Ruby's around. He wouldn't go short of female company, he told himself, as he took another pull on his drink. Yes, I'll take my pick, which is more than Ruby will be able to do when I've finished with her. No man will look at her twice

He drained his glass and motioned to the bar steward.

'Same again, sir?' the steward asked.

Stavros nodded and released a large cloud of cigar smoke across the bar. He took his drink to a table and stared into the darkness outside. The more he drank, the blacker his mood became.

It was six-thirty when the train pulled into Runcorn Station and Stavros had finished his fifth large scotch and dry. Another twenty minutes or so, he thought, as he ordered another drink. This time the steward served him in silence. He had worked the trains long enough to read people and he had no trouble noticing Stavros' changing mood.

Stavros sat at the table nursing his sixth large scotch. Yes, he thought, I'll scar her for life. She won't get another man. He could not help thinking of better times with her. Such a woman he had never had before: the shining red hair, the beautiful face, the luscious lips, the long, long legs, the large firm breasts and the swing of her hips as she walked. Maybe he would have her one more time before he destroyed her.

All of this went through his mind and as it did he hated her more, for allowing someone else to possess her. But he would have his revenge. He would leave her a wreck and then watch men ignore her. Yes, he thought, he would destroy her and enjoy it.

He looked up. The train was in Edge Hill Station. He crushed out his cigar in the ash tray and swallowed the last of his drink. He made his way to the compartment for his luggage. Five minutes, he thought, five minutes and we will be in Lime Street. Alex would be there with the car and a twenty minute drive away from Ruby.

30

Knotty Ash, Liverpool
6.15pm

The police at Derby Lane police station had taken all the details they could from Tommy, Joe and Vic. They were not to be charged, but were to report to the police station the following morning for further questioning.

Alex and Nikis were both arrested and locked up. Nikis was to be charged with grievous bodily harm and Alex for aiding and abetting. It was enough to keep them out of circulation for the immediate future. The police would, of course, oppose bail.

Ruby's description and details of the Humber were circulated.

'We'll pick her up before she gets into any more trouble,' the desk sergeant assured them, as Tommy, Joe and Vic left the station.

'Where to now?' Vic asked. 'Back to your place?'

'Not for me,' Tommy replied. 'What I want you to do now is go to the hospital. It's visiting hour, so Ma and Dad will be there. Tell them everything's OK and there won't be any more trouble. And ask Billy if he knows where Ruby went when she left the hospital.'

'And where are you going?' Joe queried.

'I'm going to Lime Street. I have an idea Ruby might show up there to meet her husband and I don't want her getting hurt.'

'Don't try anything with Stavros,' warned Vic. 'He won't fight you, he'll kill you.'

'Don't worry about me,' said Tommy. 'I just want to make sure Ruby comes out of this in one piece, for our Billy's sake.'

Joe and Vic got into the car and drove off up St. Oswald Street to Broadgreen Hospital. Tommy crossed Prescot Road and waited at the bus stop outside the builders merchants. He sheltered in the doorway and smoked a cigarette. It was dark now and was getting colder. He shivered slightly and turned up the collar of his coat, looking at his watch. It was now six-thirty. He needed a bus soon. He had to get to Lime Street station before 7 p.m. when Stavros' train was due in. Perhaps then he could keep Ruby out of trouble.

Damned Sunday service! He stamped his feet against the cold. Another look at his watch, 6-40. I'm not going to make it, he said to himself. Looking towards the lights at Derby Lane, he saw a bus approaching. Thank God, he thought. With the roads quiet, they might make it to the station in less than twenty minutes. He could still make it in time.

He boarded the bus.

'Lime Street,' he told the conductor.

'Tenp'nce,' the conductor said.

'How long?' Tommy asked as he paid.

'To Lime Street?'

'Yeah.'

The conductor shook his head. 'Not sure. This driver's no Stirling Moss. Regulation speed is what he likes. Still, we should be there in fifteen minutes or so.'

Tommy sat upstairs and the bus seemed to crawl. I can walk faster than this, he thought.

31

Liverpool City Centre
6.15pm

Ruby parked the car in Skelhorne Street. She ran onto the station concourse and checked on the London train. Platform Nine.

The ticket collector answered her without looking up. 'On time, as far as I know. Should pull in at seven o'clock.'

She ran back to the car, climbed in and started it up. Best to keep warm. She needed to be prepared for Stavros.

She had raced away from the hospital that afternoon. She felt betrayed. She felt angry. She wanted to believe that what she saw was a nurse helping a patient, but she knew what she saw. She saw Billy Walsh landing the nurse, just as he had landed her, just as the expert angler lands a fish.

So now she had nowhere to turn. Billy would always be a flirt, even if he did love her, which in his own way he probably did. He would flirt because he couldn't help it and it would eventually drive them apart.

Stavros, she knew, hated her and would want some sort of vicious retribution. When he had finished with her, he would go back for Billy and finish him off. As disappointed as she was with Billy, she wouldn't allow that.

She had driven into the city that afternoon and headed for the river. She parked the car by the Liver Buildings. It was quiet and she thought no one would think to look for her there. She left the car and walked to the waterfront. It was late afternoon and there was a cold breeze off the river. She walked for about twenty minutes as she thought of her situation and what had brought her to her present predicament.

She knew that Billy had been an opportunity to make a fresh start, but not now. She had to make her own new beginning and that meant Stavros had to be dealt with. She walked back to the small tea rooms and ordered tea and a toasted teacake. She had to decide what to do. She suddenly felt at ease with herself and realised she had not eaten or drunk anything for more than six hours. She enjoyed her refreshments and after looking at the tea room clock she made her way back to the Humber. It was five-past-six.

In the glove compartment, she found some cigarettes and lit one. She inhaled deeply as she sat composing herself, before she started the car and slowly drove to Lime Street Station.

32

6.55pm

The bus made its way down London Road at a snail's pace. Tommy was now getting anxious and as they finally approached the Odeon cinema, he decided he could not stay on the bus until it reached the stop. He ran down the stairs and as the bus slowed at the junction of London Road and Pudsey Street, he skipped off and ran for all he was worth. He turned into Pudsey Street, at the side of the cinema, where he could see the side entrance of the station in Lord Nelson Street. Looking to his left, he saw the doors of Ma Egerton's pub being opened for the evening. It's seven o'clock, he thought. Jesus Christ, I hope I'm in time!

He darted through the side gate and was on the station concourse. He ran to the nearest porter.

'The London train?' he gasped. 'Is it in yet?'

'Just arrived, mate. Platform Nine.'

Tommy could see the crowd coming through the barrier, some heading out into Lime Street and some making for the taxi rank by the Skelhorne Street exit. He did not know Stavros by sight, so he looked for Ruby.

The tannoy boomed out, taking Tommy by surprise.

'The nineteen-fifteen for Birmingham is now at platform five.'

Tommy was dodging the passengers heading for the Birmingham train and the disembarked passengers from the London train. He made it to Platform Nine and there was still a great throng of people leaving the train. There is a good chance he has not passed through the barrier yet, thought Tommy. He paused for a moment and looked about for Ruby.

He thought about Stavros. He's got to be recognisable, he said to himself. What did Vic say? 'He's a big heavy bastard and Greek.' Surely I can spot him. Tommy made his way to the ticket collector.

'Sorry to bother you, pal, but it's an emergency. I'm looking for a big fella. Greek maybe.'

The ticket collector carried on collecting tickets. 'Sorry mate, I only look at the tickets, not the faces, but some ignorant bleedin' foreigner just burst through. Looked like he'd been drinking. He was too big for me to stop. Headed for Skelhorne Street.'

'Thanks,' yelled Tommy, and he hurried towards the Skelhorne Street exit.

It was then that he saw him, big shoulders, arms akimbo, a slight waddle about his walk. He was carrying a holdall and a small suit case. His width, and the way he was carrying his luggage, meant he took up a lot of space. He wasn't moving for anyone, he just barged his way through the crowd and people who were approaching him were having to dodge him or suffer a nasty knock from his case or a holdall.

Stavros had just left the concourse and was making his way across to the taxi rank. He was looking about him, trying to spot Alex and the car, angry that Alex had not walked across to the platform to carry his bags.

He walked past the taxis and into Skelhorne Street, looking left and right. Tommy sprinted after his man. He was sure this was Stavros. He wouldn't be expecting to be tackled from behind and he would be a little worse for wear from the drink and carrying his bags. The first few blows will give me the edge, Tommy thought. He was now ten yards from him, as Stavros stood on the curb in Skelhorne Street. Three strides and he is mine, thought Tommy. He was just about to pounce, when the headlamps of an oncoming car blinded him.

33

7.05pm

Ruby had smoked three cigarettes, one after the other. She now felt ill as she looked at her watch: five-past-seven. Where is the bastard? Come on, come on, she muttered. Her elegant hands that had so attracted Billy, gripped the steering wheel. They were sweating slightly, so she rubbed them on her skirt. Don't want my hands to slip, she thought. She wiped her brow with the cuff of her jacket sleeve.

As she pulled her arm away from her face, she saw him. He was stood beneath a street light on the edge of the kerb, looking up and down Skelhorne Street. She could see the look of anger on his face. She knew what he was thinking, 'Where the fuck are you, Alex, If I say seven o'clock, you be here at seven o'clock! What do you think I pay you for, you fucking shit for brains, punch drunk has-been. Fuck me around once more, and you won't work again.' She had heard him giving Alex the payout before. She knew all of this would be going through his head as she put the big Humber into gear and pulled out into the middle of the road. Fortunately, there was no traffic about her, except for a bus making it's way to the Skelhorne Street bus station.

The driver had to brake suddenly as Ruby

swung out in front of him. There was a screech of tyres as the huge, green Leyland swerved to avoid her. People making their way to and from the railway and bus stations stopped and looked on in horror as the bus lurched, then righted itself, just missing half-a-dozen cars parked at the roadside.

Ruby neither saw nor heard a thing. She saw only Stavros.

She slipped into third gear and had reached thirty miles an hour. Her headlights were full on, cutting a white path through the murky night.

Stavros turned at the screech of tyres. He could see the headlights of the big Humber. Is this Alex, he thought, making up for lost time. No, Alex wouldn't handle the Humber like that. At the same time he was aware of someone behind him. Suddenly, he knew he was in trouble. He dropped his luggage and was about to turn, but the car headlights were close, too close. Out of the corner of his eye he saw the figure behind him dive to one side and as he looked back at the lights again, the car hit him.

Stavros was thrown thirty feet and landed on his back. He let out a deep, low groan. The drink had probably relaxed him and momentarily he tried to stand. It was only then that he felt the pain. He couldn't stand, but his instinct told him he had to try and move.

Ruby watched Stavros getting onto his knees. 'Oh shit!' she shouted out loud. She knew he was tough, but not this tough. She put the car into reverse, went back twenty yards, crashed the gear-stick into first and slammed her foot down on the accelerator. The car screeched forward, mounted the pavement and hit Stavros again. This time it flung him forward just a few feet before he crashed into the side of a waiting taxi.

Tommy rolled over on the pavement as the car hit Stavros. He looked up and saw Ruby behind the wheel. He was about to shout to her when he saw the car reverse and then rush forward, crushing Stavros against side of the taxi.

'Jesus Christ!' Tommy said, as he sat against the station wall.

The British Rail police were on the scene within seconds and a minute later the local bobbies arrived. One of the officers was making his way towards Tommy. Oh no, he thought, I don't need to be involved in this. The police officer was with a woman.

'This is the man!' she was saying as she pointed at Tommy. 'This is the man. He tried to save him. He tried to push him out of the way. I saw him, but he was too late. He was incredibly brave!'

'Well done, son,' another police officer said. 'Pity you couldn't have got to him a couple of seconds earlier.'

Tommy looked at him and reached into his pocket for a cigarette. He put one between his lips.

'Got a light?' he asked the policeman.

'We'll need you for a statement,' the constable said, as he passed him a box of matches. 'Don't go away just yet. You get yourself a cuppa and I'll be along to talk to you shortly.'

Tommy stood and watched as Ruby was taken from the car.

She looked calm and poised, as though she had carried out a great deed. She didn't appear to notice him. Maybe she didn't want to. She just looked straight ahead as the police led her away. An ambulance arrived, followed by a fire engine.

'They're going to have to cut him out of that mess,' Tommy heard someone say.

'Is he dead?' said another.

'Not 'alf!' said a third. 'She near cut him in two.'

Tommy lifted the cigarette to his lips and saw his hand was shaking. Time I wasn't here, he said to himself. Quite a crowd had gathered and he slipped away unnoticed through the mass. He made his way to Lime Street and flagged a cab.

'Where to, wack?' asked the cabbie.

'Broadgreen Hospital,' Tommy said as he sank back into the seat.

'Just come from the station have you?' enquired the cabbie.

'Er, no, why?' answered Tommy.

'Oh, some bird has just gone berserk,' said the cabbie. 'Drove her car into the station. Tried to kill everyone in sight, she did. Some fella tried to stop her, but he got flung out of the way.'

'Oh, you never know the day,' said Tommy

34

8pm

Ward-sister Wilson had a forgiving nature and was more understanding than Sister Pringle, so when Tommy told her he had just arrived home on leave from Aldershot, she was only too pleased to allow him onto the ward to see Billy.

'Only thirty minutes mind!' she warned. 'Don't want to upset the rest of the patients.'

'Thanks sister,' said Tommy, and he made his way to Billy's bed.

Billy saw him coming and knew it was bad news. He knew Tommy, Joe and Vic were OK, but he knew there would be bad news about Ruby. As Tommy reached him, Billy started to fill up, his eyes glistened and he had to swallow hard.

'Hi, kid, everyone OK?'

Tommy sat down and put a hand on Billy's shoulder. 'It's over, Billy, but it didn't turn out right.'

'It's Ruby, isn't it? She's in trouble.' Billy answered his own question.

'She killed Stavros,' Tommy said. He watched as Billy stiffened as though he had been electrocuted. 'I thought she might do something stupid, Billy, but I couldn't stop her.' He looked down at his brother and shook his head. 'You've been in some scrapes over women, but this takes the biscuit.'

Billy told Tommy about the Nurse Watson incident.

'Bleeding hell, Billy. Don't you know when to stop?'

'I couldn't help it,' Billy protested. 'It just happened. It always happens when I least expect it. Anyway, Nurse Watson wants to help me recover and she is not married or courting.'

'I don't believe I'm hearing this,' Tommy said, exasperated. 'What about Ruby? You told me you'd fallen for her good style?'

'Tommy, she was fabulous. You don't know how good she was. I told her I loved her and I do. But I don't think she'll want to know me now. I think that's why she did what she did.'

Tommy found a towel and wiped Billy's eyes and forehead.

'So what are you going to do?' he asked him.

'I don't know,' Billy said, 'I'll try and get in touch with her, but I think it's over.'

Tommy got up to leave.

'I'm going home to tell Ma and Dad that everyone's safe. Ma'll be pleased. She hasn't had much to smile about in the last twenty-four hours.'

Billy reached out and gripped Tommy's arm.

'I'm sorry, Tom,' he said hoarsely. 'Tell Ma and Dad and the boys I'm sorry. I didn't think it would lead to all this trouble.' His eyes began to water.

'See you tomorrow,' Tommy said, patting Billy's arm as he stood up to leave. 'You get some sleep.'

Queenie, Jack, Vic, Joe and the girls were sitting around the kitchen table when Tommy arrived home. Tommy related the events at the station and the subsequent visit to the hospital.

'Our Billy's a strange bugger,' he said. 'He took it really hard when I told him about Ruby, but then he tells me about this nurse who's going to look after him. At least she isn't married.'

'I'll speak to that Billy,' Jack said. 'He doesn't know what he's put us through.'

'Now, now Jack,' chided Queenie. 'Let's be grateful things didn't turn out any worse. At least we are still all here, still one family.'

35

Piccadilly, London
Monday Morning
9 o' clock

In Panton Street, opposite the Tom Cribb public house, a busy little breakfast bar was coping with the morning rush.

'Egg on toast, darlin',' said Maggie Kelly, proprietor, as she placed the order down in front of the blonde sitting on the high stool at the end of the bar.

The blonde was reading the Daily Mirror and appeared not to hear Maggie.

'You in love or somethin', darlin'?' Maggie said, and tapped the blonde's arm.

'Oh, sorry, Maggie,' the blonde replied, 'I was well away. I just spotted something in the Stop Press and it shook me up a bit.'

The blonde folded the paper and laid it on the bar. She took a sip of her tea and picked up a piece of toast. She folded the half slice of bread in two and dipped a corner of it into her egg. She took a bite and began to chew. She swallowed and dipped the toast into the egg again. She raised it to her mouth, then stopped. She put the toast back on the plate and pushed it away from her and then she began to shake.

Maggie returned. 'You sure you're all right,

darlin'? You 'ardly touched your breakfast.'

'I'll be OK Maggie,' the blonde said. 'I'm just going for a walk. I'll be back later for a cuppa.'

She stepped out into Panton Street and walked towards Piccadilly Circus. It must be what they call poetic justice, she thought, and her step lightened and a smile lit up her face.

Maggie Kelly shook her head as she scrapped the egg and toast off the plate. She picked up the newspaper to see what it was that caused her customer to act so strangely that she couldn't finish her breakfast. She looked at the Stop Press.

WOMAN CHARGED WITH MURDER

Stavros Ziacos, 30, a local businessman, was hit by a car and killed on Sunday evening at Liverpool's Lime Street Station. A 27-year-old woman, believed to be his wife, has been arrested and charged with murder. The police are appealing for witnesses.

Well, these prostitutes get around, Maggie thought to herself, but surely Paula doesn't know anyone in Liverpool.

36

Broadgreen Hospital,
Liverpool
9.30am

Mr Mackintosh was the orthopaedic surgeon who had operated on Billy's ankles on Sunday morning. He was now doing his rounds. He swept into ward D4, followed by two junior doctors, Matron Harris and Sister Pringle. The cortège eventually reached Billy.

'Well, how are we this morning?' asked Mr Mackintosh, in a soft Scottish burr.

'All things considered, not too bad, doctor,' Billy replied. 'But my ribs are still sore and my ankles ache.'

'Well, your ankles will knit, given time, as they'll be in plaster for at least six weeks. Your ribs, however, are only strapped, so you'll have to move about as little as possible. You should feel a lot better over the next seven days. Then we will see about getting you out of bed for a few hours each day.'

'When do you think I'll be able to start walking again?' asked Billy.

'Don't be in a hurry,' replied the surgeon. 'If you try too soon, you might set yourself back, so we won't be looking for a quick cure here. When I think you're ready, we'll get the physiotherapist to plan a routine aimed at getting you walking again. But all in good time. Any other problems?'

'Well,' Billy murmured, 'there is something I need to know, just for my own peace of mind.'

'And that is?'

'You see . . . ' Billy struggled to get the words out, knowing in his heart what the answer would be.

'Come on, Mr Walsh,' chivvied Sister Pringle. 'Mr Mackintosh hasn't got all day. He has other patients to see.'

The surgeon held up his hand to Sister Pringle, motioning her to let Billy take his time.

'Now, Mr Walsh, what's troubling you?'

Billy stuttered. 'I . . . I like to dance. It's the one thing I'm really good at. I'm a good dancer. The women, well, they like to dance with me and that's my sort of routine when I meet them. So what I'm really asking, I suppose, is will I be able to dance again?'

Mr Mackintosh stroked his chin. 'Well, what can I say? I don't see why you shouldn't be able to manage the occasional waltz, but that's about it, I would guess.'

'No tango?' spluttered Billy. 'It's the only dance worth doing. The waltz isn't a dance. I don't waltz, I tango. You're having me on.'

'I'm sorry, Mr Walsh, but if you want to be able to walk when you're an older man and be free from arthritis for as long as possible, my advice to you is convince yourself that you have danced your last tango.' With that, Mr

Mackintosh, and his escort left the ward.

Billy lay on his bed, staring at the ceiling. He couldn't believe it. He was dumbstruck.

For the rest of the morning he was depressed. It was going to be difficult coming to terms with the events of the weekend and the coup-de-gras was the surgeon's pronouncement.

At noon, Linda came on duty. She visited each patient in turn, making sure they were settled and had all taken their respective medication. She left Billy until the last, so she could spend more time with him. Finally, she came to him. She gave him his painkillers and fixed his ankle supports, fluffed up his pillows and sat by his bed. Sister Pringle had gone to lunch, so it would be quiet for the next hour or so.

Billy told her about the surgeon's visit and she sympathised with him. She took his hand, stroked it and told him she would be strong for him.

Billy was feeling better already.

'Do you know what I'd like you to do for me when I get out of here?' he said.

'Anything you want, you ask and I'll do it,' she answered.

'Well,' Billy said, 'I want you to teach me how to waltz.

Book Two

37

April
Friday
7.20pm

For the fifth time in as many minutes, Linda looked at her watch. Billy was late. He was always late. In fact, once or twice he had failed to turn up at all and as the minutes passed, she was beginning to think this was another occasion he would let her down.

She cursed herself. She should have known better right at the beginning. She was stupid getting involved with him. What made it harder to take was that she knew instinctively from the start that a relationship with him was doomed to failure.

It was now six weeks since he had left hospital. At least whilst he was an in-patient, she had been able to keep an eye on him. But not anymore. In fact, the moment he had mastered his crutches he started to wander. It wasn't unusual to find him on the ladies wards chatting up other nurses.

She sighed to herself and decided to give him five more minutes then she was getting the bus home and forgetting all about Billy Walsh.

It was that day in the ward, as she comforted him, when the red-headed woman appeared and she heard Billy gasp her name. 'Ruby! Ruby!' He had spoken hoarsely, hardly audible, and as she turned to look she saw Ruby, hand to mouth, turn and run. She knew then that it was folly to form any sort of relationship with him, but he was a sweet talker and he needed her. He was badly injured with damaged ankles, cracked by a hammer in the hands of Ruby's husband's henchmen.

She now stood tapping her feet. A petite figure, her auburn hair in a pony tail bobbed as her foot rapped out a beat of annoyance. Another five minutes, she said to herself, then, don't be a bloody fool. Go home. She checked her watch again: seven-thirty. Too late for the cinema now, she thought. She had been waiting for forty-five minutes at the junction of Prescot Street and Kensington, outside the Sacred Heart church.

'We'll have a drink and walk along to the Majestic,' Billy had said. Look Back in Anger starring Richard Burton was showing and Billy had heard it was a good film.

She let out a sigh, and controlling her anger she crossed the junction and walked along Kensington to the bus stop. That's it, she thought, that's bloody it! No more Billy Walsh and if he has the nerve to turn up at the hospital on Monday, I'll tell him to get out of my life.

She stood at the bus stop and there was a trace of a tear in her eyes as she recalled the hectic three months they had spent together. The memories came flooding back thick and fast: how she had comforted him as he recovered from the beating and the shock he was in on being informed his broken ankles would mean he would never dance his beloved tango again.

She recalled the hours she had spent with him, both on and off duty and how eventually he had come to terms with his injuries, only to be set back mentally when he heard Ruby had been jailed for twelve years for the manslaughter of her abusive husband. Although he never went into detail, she knew he had loved Ruby. Linda had been his crutch throughout all this and what had she got out of it? Nothing.

Billy's ankles were scarcely out of plaster and she was on night duty when it happened the first time. She remembered how he hobbled to the empty ward at one o'clock in the morning. He may not have been able to walk too well, but once in bed he was as good as anyone. What was it he said? A bed is a great leveller.

He had taken her gently, caressing her body, kissing her neck and shoulders as he unbuttoned her blouse.

'You're a sensual woman, Linda,' he whispered into her ear. She recalled moaning as he cupped her breasts and let his tongue flick over her nipples. She told him what he wanted to hear.

'I love you, Billy,' she gasped out as she untied his dressing gown. Billy was naked and one glance told her that he was ready for her. She reached for him and he found her. When they were ready, Linda had to do the work. Billy lay back and guided her onto him. She was new to this openness in lovemaking, but he made her feel at ease. He guided her to a shuddering climax

'Linda, you've made a wounded man very happy,' he told her. 'I'm lucky to have found you and now I'm going to keep you.'

She fell for it hook, line and sinker and as the weeks passed, Billy was as attentive as ever when he wanted sex and off hand once he was satisfied. That was when she noticed him talking to other nurses. Not just talking, but paying them a good deal of attention.

'Lin, you're the one for me,' he would plead. 'Don't I owe you everything? You are the love of my life.'

Soon the time came for him to be discharged. They had been out a number of times for a drink or a movie and they usually went back to her flat in Eaton Road, where Billy would spend the night. Lately, however, he had been late or not turned up and she knew he was tiring of her. He'd had all he wanted.

The bus arrived and Linda boarded it.

'Eaton Road, please,' she said to the conductor.

'Tenp'nce, love,' he said and flicked a ticket out of his machine.

She took a seat and as the bus left the stop, she looked out of the window and saw her reflection in the evening light. She saw a tear running down her cheek and felt sad, and used. Damn you, Billy Walsh, she thought to herself, damn you! The next time I see you I'll give you a piece of my mind and you can stay out of my life forever.

38

7.40pm

The girl in the high heels and tight skirt nearly overbalanced as she tentatively negotiated the two steep steps from the pub doorway to the street level. She was giggling as she put out a hand to assist her companion, who with the help of a walking stick found the steps just as awkward to descend.

'Oh, Billy, is that stick going to get in the way of everything tonight?' she asked him.

'I don't need it for what I've got in mind,' Billy replied.

'Billy Walsh, you dirty old man!' Carol shrieked.

'Less of the old,' Billy warned with a laugh. 'You're only eight years younger than me. Anyway, didn't I promise you a good night in, later?

'Shush, Billy. People will hear you.'

'I don't care who hears me when I'm with the most exciting woman I know.' Billy held his arms out and Carol stepped into them. He pulled her close and kissed her. An elderly couple, making their way into the Coach and Horses pub were watching.

'Disgusting people!' the woman snorted.

'Lucky bugger!' the man murmured.

Billy looked across Kensington towards the corner of Hall Lane. That's where Linda would have waited, he thought, outside the Sacred Heart church. He was fairly confident she wouldn't be there now, not at a quarter to eight. He had said seven o'clock and he knew she would give up and go home. I'll sweet talk her on Monday when I go to the hospital for physio, he thought, and he felt a small pang of regret for standing her up. But then he looked at Carol as she stood on tip toe and kissed him and nurse Linda Watson was forgotten about.

'Penny for your thoughts,' Carol said.

'Oh, nothing to worry your pretty little head about,' Billy replied.

'Is it the injury?' she persisted. 'I can't believe those two brutes would pick on you just because you were a good dancer and you showed them up.'

'Well, jealousy is a nasty thing,' Billy said. He had failed to tell Carol he was in bed with their boss's wife at the time.

'I'm glad you came back to the pub,' she said. 'When you called in just after New Year, you said you'd be in again a few days later and I was looking forward to it. But I'd given up after three months.

'Well, like I told you this afternoon, I would have been back sooner except for this little accident. Six weeks I've been in Broadgreen Hospital and six weeks as an out-patient for physiotherapy. I couldn't do anything,' Billy lied.

'Couldn't go anywhere. So I'm glad I called in this afternoon and you were able to change your night off. I really need your company, Carol.'

'Poor Billy,' Carol purred, as she stroked his hair, 'You've been through such a lot and I'm going to take care of you and get you back into the land of the living. So where are we going?'

'Before we go back to your place?' Billy asked mischievously.

'Of course,' said Carol. 'Let's at least enjoy a few drinks first.'

'Then back to your place?' Billy asked again.

'Now don't keep asking or you may not get. It is my night off, so let's visit a couple of pubs, then you can take me home by taxi and I'll see you're rewarded.'

Billy winced. Visit a few pubs. Taxi home. His sick pay from Cunard was running low. He had hoped that a couple of Babychams in the Coach and Horses might have done the trick, but he hadn't allowed for the fact that Carol was a barmaid and a couple of Babychams was water off a ducks back.

Oh well, he thought, in for a penny. I hope she's worth it. Carol was attractive, with bobbed fair hair and a small nose which gave her a cheeky look. She was so slim her waist could only have been about eighteen inches. Her breasts were small but perfectly formed. He looked at her legs and the high heels made them look quite shapely. Billy weighed it all up and decided she would be worth it.

'Let's go to the Blue Ball then,' he suggested. 'There's usually live music on tonight. Then maybe we could go to the Legs of Man. Ever try the Cocktail Bar there?'

Carol moved closer to him. 'Now that sounds good,' she enthused. She reached for his face and pulled it to hers and kissed him, her tongue darting into his mouth.

He was surprised at how fierce the kiss was and as he tried to respond, she pushed him away.

'Don't go getting too excited now, Billy,' she teased. 'Save it for later. Meanwhile, let's go and have some fun. She linked his arm and they set off across Low Hill to Prescot Street and the Blue Ball. Suddenly, Billy was managing to walk without the constant use of his stick and his mind was working overtime. Don't drink too much. Plenty of lemonade in the Highballs. Watch Carol doesn't overdo the Babycham, or the lager and lime. This could be worth waiting for. Don't want to fluff it.

As they reached the pub he fairly skipped up the steps.

38

8.pm

As Linda walked along Eaton Road towards her flat, her hurt was turning more to anger. Where does that flash bastard think he's getting off? She asked herself. Now she thought about it, she remembered catching him chatting-up the physiotherapist only a couple of days ago. She'll find out what he's like the hard way.

And what about this Ruby who made such an impression on him? He would never be drawn when her name was mentioned, but she had obviously meant a lot to him once. Maybe, Linda thought, she had tried to hard to take this woman's place, trying too hard to be somebody that she wasn't. Maybe that was where she went wrong.

I went wrong. The only thing wrong with this relationship, she decided, was Billy bloody Walsh.

She reached Alder Hey hospital and crossed the road to the flat she shared with another nurse. She had the first-floor of a semi-detached house and Sally Redmond had the ground-floor. Linda wondered if he had ever tried it on with Sally. He might have called round unannounced one day and found Sally alone.

I'm going mad with this, she wondered, suspecting even her friends were seeing Billy behind her back.

She opened the front-door and went upstairs. At the top of the stairs was another door leading to her flat. As she entered, she switched on the light and surveyed her empty home. It was not the same without him. Especially now she knew she was going to finish it.

She felt depressed. She would, she knew, miss his noise, his laugh, his off-beat ways and his little throwaway compliments. 'You look gorgous tonight,' he used to say. 'You've got beautiful hair.' 'I love your legs.' 'I could look at you all day.' 'I'm so lucky I met you.'

When they made love on the carpet with the windows open, they could hear the noise of the traffic around the children's hospital. 'We can hear everything that's going on,' he'd say, 'but all those people out there don't know I'm making love to a beautiful woman in here.' All words. Just words.

When they made love, she stifled her cries as she reached her orgasm in case the people below thought she was being murdered. Now, she walked over to the bed, kicked off her shoes and threw her face onto her pillow. She sobbed without restraint. Let the world hear how heart-broken and miserable she was.

In the Blue Ball pub, the group had just finished playing Blackboard of my Heart. Carol had been tapping her feet and clicking her fingers for the past half-an-hour. Hank Walters and the Dusty Road Ramblers had played a succession of Country and

Western hits including Your Cheating Heart, Hey Good Lookin' and Howling at the Moon.

It wasn't all to Billy's taste. He preferred the big ballads and the smooth sweep of an orchestra, though Hank and his group were tolerable. More to the point, Carol loved it and he was after keeping her as sweet as he could.

'Let's take a walk to the Legs of Mann,' Billy suggested. 'And perhaps the American Bar. Then we go for a curry in Bold Street, if you like.'

'Sounds good to me,' Carol said.

Ten minutes later they were sat in the Cocktail Bar of the Legs of Mann.

'I've never had a proper cocktail,' Carol confessed.

'Well, now's your chance,' Billy said, catching the waiter's eye. He ordered a Highball for himself and a Harvey Wallbanger for Carol.

'What's a Harvey Wallbanger?' she asked with a juvenile smile.

'Taste it and see.'

When the drinks came, she lifted the exotic looking concoction to her lips, but hesitated. 'I'm not sure about this,' she said.

'Don't be a stick in the mud,' Billy said, teasing her. 'Just try it. Life's more exiting when you take a little risk. You can't spend your entire life drinking Babycham and lager.'

She still hesitated.

Billy shook his head, smiling. 'I can't promise this will be the defining moment of your life, but it's something different. Drink it.'

'You're a bleedin' philosopher, you are, Billy Walsh!' Carol giggled. 'You've talked me into it.'

The waiter placed the drink in front of her and Billy raised his Highball, inviting carol to touch glasses.

'Cheers!' she said, with a laugh.

'To us,' Billy responded.

Carol took a cautious sip and allowed the drink to linger on her palate. 'Mmm! Not bad at all!' she exclaimed. 'I could get used to this.'

'Well,' Billy said, 'drink that and we'll have another one. Then we'll go and have that curry. I'm starving and I'll need to keep my strength up for later.' He gave her a knowing smile.

'I hope you've got plenty of staying power, Billy,' she said. 'You're going to need it!'

Linda woke up in her dark, dreary bedroom and looked at her watch: eleven o'clock. She stretched and yawned. 'Damn,' she muttered. She had found it difficult to go to sleep in the first place. Now, with the edge taken off her tiredness, it would be almost impossible. Her stomach tightened as she recalled the reason for her early night. Bloody Billy Walsh! Her lips trembled, but she swung her legs out of the bed and was determined to get a grip of herself. 'No more tears,' she whispered.

If sleep was beyond her, she decided, then the best therapy was a good soak in the bath. She went into the bathroom and turned on the hot tap. Taking off her blouse and skirt, she let them drop to the floor. Her bra and knickers followed. She turned to look at herself in the cabinet-mirror on the wall.

Maybe I'm just too plain for him, she thought. He used me when he couldn't get about on his shattered ankles. Now he was more mobile, he's got no time for me. I'm not bad looking, but I don't use enough make-up. Good figure, good legs, but maybe I don't strut my stuff the way he likes it.

'Well, I think you look pretty good, Linda Watson,' she said aloud as she stepped into the bath.

On the corner of Hanover Street and Bold Street, Billy looked out for a cab as Carol held onto his arm.

'That was a lovely night,' she said. 'You certainly know how to give a girl a good time.'

'I'm glad you enjoyed yourself. What did you think of the curry?'

'It was different.'

'Not keen, then?' Billy asked, smiling.

'No, it was great, but I've never had a proper Indian curry before. It was bleedin' hot!'

Billy laughed. 'You'd try another one?'

'You bet,' she answered. 'As long as you're with me.'

Billy flagged a passing cab and pulled at the kerbside in front of them. As they settled in, Carol leaned forward to speak to the driver. 'Newsham Drive, please, mate.'

As she sat back, Billy put his arm around her shoulders and she rested her head on his chest.

'Happy?' he asked.

'Mmm,' she answered.

'You could be happier.'

'How?'

'If I made you a night-cap when we get back to your place.'

'Can't wait,' she purred.

What am I going to do? Linda thought, as she dried herself off. I could pluck my eyebrows and ask Sally to give me a perm. She used to be a hairdresser before she was a nurse. Maybe she would tell me what make-up I should be using. Yes, that's what I need. A new image!

She walked back into the bedroom and put on her night-dress. She climbed into bed and felt better with herself now she had resolved to do something positive. I'll see Sally first thing in the morning, she thought. I'll show him. You see. He'll see what he's missing.

Suddenly at peace with herself, she felt tired. Laying her head down, she was asleep within a minute.

Carol's spacious second-floor flat had a large living room with a bay window that overlooked Newsham Park. There was also a single bedroom, kitchen and bathroom.

'This is cosy,' Billy said, looking about him.

There was a large rug in the centre of the

polished floorboards and although sparsely furnished, it looked comfortable. There was no settee, just two large leather armchairs and a long low coffee table. The flat was heated by a single gas fire.

To either side of the chimney breast was a small recess. On the right was a gramophone, but Billy's attention was attracted to the considerable record collection on the left. Four shelves were crammed with records.

'Wow! You never said you collected records.'

'I don't really,' she said. 'They're not mine. Well, they are now, but I didn't collect them.'

'Who did?'

'Ryan.' She turned to the kitchen 'I'll make us a cup of tea.'

'Who's Ryan?'

'Ryan Elwood,' she shouted from the kitchen. 'A Yank. He was an hydraulics expert stationed at the base in Burtonwood. He used to test the arrester-gear used by US Navy planes when they land on aircraft carriers.'

'Fascinating,' Billy answered dryly. 'How did you meet him?'

'I was invited to a dance at Burtonwood. We clicked straight away.'

'How long did it last?'

'Three years.'

'When did you split up?'

'We didn't really "split up". He just took off. He had a five-year lease on this place and we lived here together until six months ago. Then he left me a note saying, "Sorry. Got to go back Stateside. It's been great. Probably won't be back. Stay in the flat until the lease is up." And that was it. There's still eighteen months left on the lease and I'm in no hurry to move.'

'Sounds like you miss him,' Billy asked cautiously.

'Did at first. He used to throw great parties. That's what all the records were for. There used to be dozens of people all over the floor, dancing and snogging. In the summer, the parties used to spill out into the garden. It's certainly been a lot quieter since he went.'

'Has there been anyone else since?'

'Not until you.'

The kettle started to whistle and a moment later Carol came back into the living room with two cups of tea.

Billy looked through the records. There were plenty of Hank Williams, Hank Locklain and Hank Snow. Some Patsy Cline and Jim Reeves. The thought struck Billy that carol must have been reminded of Ryan when Hank Waters and the Dusty Road Ramblers were playing in the Blue Ball. It was the same music.

He thought something romantic was appropriate and picked out Come Softly to Me and Mr Blue by The Fleetwoods, Lonely Boy by Paul Anka and Venus by Frankie Avalon.

Carol took the records from him and walked to the gramophone. 'Pass me two more,' she said. 'It'll take six at a time.' She went through the records he had chosen. 'Get Heartaches by the Number by Guy Mitchell and Smoke Gets in Your Eyes by The Platters.'

A moment later, the first record dropped onto the turntable and the voice of Paul Anka filled the room.

I'm just a lonely boy,
Lonely and Blue.

'Good choice,' Carol said.

When the song finished, the next record, Come Softly to Me, dropped down the spindle and began to play.

'Very appropriate,' she said.

Billy nodded and took her into his arms. They kissed passionately, breaking only when the record finished and silence descended on the room.

'I'm ready for that Billy Walsh night-cap now,' she said, and led him towards the bedroom.

40

Saturday
9.30am

Billy ground out his cigarette as the bus approached the Newsham Park gates on Prescot Road. It had been a good night, but against his better judgement he had agreed to see her again that night. He was to pick he up just after ten when she finished work in the Red House. He had been hoping to slip out of the flat before she woke, but wake she did and extracted from him a promise to take her out.

Initially, he had tried to get out of it, but she wasn't playing.

'If you think you can have one night in bed with me on the strength of a few drinks and a curry, think again!' she said, with no little venom in her tongue.

He decided he would have to spend with the weekend with carol, but if he got word to Linda that he was busy with something, he could pick up the threads of that next week. He was sure she would forgive him. She always did. Come Monday, he was seeing the Cunard doctor and was hoping to get his old job back on the Sylvania. He could then wave goodbye to Carol from the safety of the ship.

He would make it up to Linda with a night out

next Saturday at the Rialto luxury ballroom. It was always a good night with Hal Graham and his Broadcasting Orchestra. In the meantime, he had to keep carol sweet.

'See you at ten o'clock,' she said as he left. 'And don't be late.'

Linda pushed her bicycle out of the front gate and peddled off along Eaton Road towards the shops on East Prescot Road. It was twenty to ten and the road was quiet. She needed milk and bread and something for the Sunday dinner, maybe pork chops. She had also decided to buy a Toni Home Perm. After consulting with Sally, she had decided to lighten her hair colour and Sally was going to do it for her that afternoon. Sally had lifted her spirits and tried to convince her that Billy was not the most important thing in her world.

As she peddled close to the kerb, a pus passed her and pulled up at the bus stop twenty yards in front of her. A couple of passengers stepped off and the conductor rang the bell. Linda slowed to a stop and looked up.

Looking back at her was Billy. By the look on his face, she was the last person he had expected to see. His jaw dropped and he was obviously trying to mouth some form of apology.

She glared back at him and shook her head. He stood up and tried to make his way to the boarding platform as the bus pulled away, but hampered by his ankles, he stumbled and fell back into one of the bench seats. By the time he

grabbed the pole at the back of the bus, they were
going too fast and he couldn't jump down.
Instead, he called out to her.

'Linda! I'm sorry! I got caught up with friends!
I'll ring you! Explain everything!'

The conductor put an arm on his shoulder. 'You
can't organise your love-life standing their, mate.
You'll break your neck.' He looked down at Billy's
ankles. 'Is that what happened last time?' he joked.
'Sit down. If she loves you, she'll forgive you.'

Billy watched Linda as the bus pulled further
and further away. 'Did you see the expression on
her face? I don't think she will.'

Linda heard 'sorry' and 'friends' and something
about getting 'in touch'. She thought he looked a
bit dishevelled, as if he'd been out all night. She
tried to smile. He probably bloody had.

Carol was not due in the pub until five-thirty and
after taking a bath decided to call in on her dad.
He always looked forward to visits, not least
because she always did some cleaning and ironing
for him.

Jimmy Roberts had found housework difficult
since his left hand was crushed under a pallet of
whisky that had slipped from its sling when being
loaded into a ship's hold. He hadn't worked since.
The man he blamed, who was guiding the load,
was finished on the docks too. He had tried to lift
the pallet off Jimmy and had ripped the muscles
in his back.

They had not been friends before the accident

and Jimmy found it easy to blame him. He was convinced the man had done it on purpose and only tried to help him because he hadn't killed him. He had to be seen to be doing something when he lay trapped and in agony. He promised himself he would get even one day

Carol suffered her father's bitterness in silence. His surliness meant he had few friends and since her mother had died three years ago, he had had to fend for himself. Carol did what she could to help and called on him at least once a week. They had little in common and little to talk about, but she decided she would tell him about Billy. Her father had never approved of Ryan and seemed to enjoy the moment she had told him he had gone for good.

He didn't say anything, but she saw the words in his eyes: 'Told you so. Yanks are all the same.'

Linda could not get Billy out of her mind and was tormented by thoughts of where he might have spent the night and, more to the point, who he was with. Obviously with a woman, she thought. She tried to console herself with the fact that she had only known him for three months and they were hardly engaged to be married, but it didn't work.

She already loved him. She knew it. He was the first man to truly arouse her, the first to give her real sexual pleasure. She only wanted to be with him. The hours when they were apart were like a vacuum which she filled as best she could, counting down the hours until she was with him again. He was fun to be with, he took her to the best restaurants and, when he turned up, he treated her like a lady.

She shook her head. 'Forget him, forget him, forget him! He will drive you mad!' but she would go insane without him. It didn't matter what he did. She couldn't help herself. She loved him. Damn! Damn! Damn!

There was a knock on the door and she opened it to let Sally in.

Sally gave her friend a compassionate smile when she saw the shadows beneath her eyes. 'That bad, eh?'

'Oh, you know me,' she answered bravely. 'Blubber over the least little thing.'

'What happened? Had a row?'

'I wish,' Linda answered. 'I didn't see him to have a row with. He stood me up again.'

'Get rid of him, Linda. He's no good for you.'

'I can't help it. I love him.'

Sally glanced across at her. 'The last woman who fell in love with your Billy Walsh ended up killing her husband and going to jail.'

'I know.'

'Let's have a cup of tea and see what we can do to cheer you up.'

Linda remembered the perm. 'I've bought myself a Toni Home Perm.'

Sally looked at her friend and smiled. 'Good. You're very pretty, Linda, but you don't do enough with what you've got. Why don't we give you a new image?'

'I'm glad you said that,' Linda replied. 'That might keep Billy interested.'

41

3.30pm

Carol walked up the path of her father's council house in Page Moss Avenue and saw the television was on. Jimmy Roberts was watching the wrestling: Billy Two Rivers, the Red Indian, Big Jim Hussey and Honey Boy Zimba. Before his accident, her father used to go down to the Liverpool Stadium to watch the wrestling every Friday night, but now he had to settle for the TV coverage.

He answered her knock in his usual brusque manner. 'I thought you weren't coming. You're usually here buy lunchtime.'

Carol felt her irritation rising, but held it back. 'I was out late last night and slept in. But I'll go home if you want.'

'All right, all right,' he snapped back. 'I'll make a brew before you start.'

Carol went straight to the kitchen and put up the ironing board, then stacked her father's washing on a chair. On the television, the commentator, Ken Walton, was introducing the next bout, a 'real treat' between Jackie Pallo and Bert Royle.

'He's a dirty bugger, that Pallo,' he father called out. 'He'll be fouling Royle and conning the ref from start to finish.'

'Don't be daft, Dad,' Carol said. 'It's fixed. Everyone knows it's fixed.'

'Rubbish,' Jimmy responded. 'I've seen these fellas at the Stadium. They don't mess about.'

Let him believe what he wants, she thought. She took a sip of her tea and touched the iron with a wet finger. It hissed back at her. She picked up the first of the seven shirts waiting to be ironed, one for each day of the week. Jimmy was nothing if not smart.

A little more than an hour later, the ironing was finished and Carol prepared some chopped ham, tomatoes and beetroot for their tea. As she set out the table, the wrestling finished and the television teleprinter began to spit out the first of the day's football results. Everton, in the First Division, lost 3-2 to West Ham united at Upton Park. Liverpool, in the Second Division, beat Derby County 3-0 at Anfield.

Jimmy, an Evertonian, switched off the set in disappointment and turned to face his daughter. 'So it's a new boyfriend then?' he asked.

'What makes you think that,' Carol said defensively.

'Because your night off is usually a Monday and you wouldn't bother swapping it unless a fella was involved.'

'You've been watching too many episodes of Boyd QC and Murder Bag, but if you must know, yes, I have met someone.'

'Not another bloody married Yank, I hope!' Jimmy barked.

'Don't start off on that again, Dad. Anyway, Billy Walsh is a local lad. He lives in Knotty Ash and sails with Cunard.'

'A merchant navy man, eh?' Jimmy said, a sarcastic sneer crossing his face. 'Probably got a girl in every port.'

Carol sighed. 'Do you have to find fault with everyone I meet?' She prepared to leave. 'I'm determined to keep this one, Dad, so if you don't mind, I'll be on my way. I want to get to work early, so I can leave handy. Billy's taking me to the Cavern to see the Alex Welsh Jazz Band. He hasn't been there before, but he seemed to like Hank Walters last night.'

As she made her way to the front door, her father called after her. 'Just a minute. Did you say Billy Walsh?'

'Yes. What about it?'

'Probably nothing. I knew a fella on the docks called Walsh who lived over in Knotty Ash.'

'Well, it wasn't Billy. He been going away to sea since he left school. Maybe it was his Dad. What was his name?'

'Jack.'

'Okay, I'll find out.'

'You do that,' Jimmy said quietly as Carol closed the door behind her.

She made her way to Pilch lane and waited for the bus. She was close to the Ashfield Dairy Farm, where she worked on a milk round just after the war. She was fifteen and still a tomboy. Phil, the dairyman, taught her to drive the horse and cart. She loved the work and wouldn't listen to her parents' pleas to get a job more appropriate for a 'young lady' in Woolworths, Lewis's or TJ Hughes's. Her older sister, Pauline, worked as a line supervisor at the Automatic on Edge Lane.

While she was 'on the milk' she met Kenny Reynolds and began spending her free afternoons in his bedroom when his parents were out working. Almost inevitably, Carol became pregnant. After furious arguments and endless tears, they married quickly at the St Margaret Mary's Church and Carol moved in with Kenny's parents.

The marriage was a huge mistake and when Carol miscarried in the fifth month of her pregnancy, she packed her bags and went to stay with her sister. Pauline had married well and was living in a large house in Prospect Vale in Fairfield, but to help pay her way, carol took a job as a barmaid in the Fairfield Arms. She was made for the job.

In time, she was able to afford her own flat over a Draper's shop in Prescot Road and it was there she finally celebrated her divorce. She moved on to the Red House when offered the job of head-barmaid and it was there she met Ryan and left her flat in Prescot Road for Newsham Park.

The bus finally came and dropped her off at Broadgreen Road in Old Swan.

Billy climbed out of the bath and reached for the towel. The bathroom was cold after the warmth of

187

the water and his teeth chattered as he briskly towelled himself down. He felt warmer as he pulled on a clean white T-shirt and briefs. After five hours sleep, he felt better and all he needed now a cup of tea and a bite to eat. He would look through the Liverpool Echo to see which band was playing at which venue.

Bobby was sitting in the kitchen with Dave, strumming a battered guitar. They were working vainly on the chords of It Doesn't Matter Anymore, the current chart-topper by Buddy Holly. Billy thought it sounded awful and after pouring himself a cup of tea, suggested they take a break.

'Go and get the Echo from the living room for me, Bobby,' Billy asked.

'Yer'll have to wait,' Bobby answered. 'Me dad's listening to the football results and checking his pools coupon. He's using the fixtures in the Echo to write the scores down.'

Bobby and Dave returned to the job in hand and Billy sighed with exasperation.

'Listen, boys,' he said. 'That's not music. You can't compare plunking on cat gut with the sound made by a full string and wind orchestra.'

Bobby responded without looking up. 'You know your trouble, Billy? You're a square.'

Dave nodded in agreement. 'Bobby's right. Rock 'n' Roll is the scene now. It's all Buddy Holly, Elvis Presley, Cliff Richard and Bobby Darren. Bands and orchestras are out, Billy.'

Billy smiled and shook his head. 'Whatever you say, lads, but when everybody's forgotten about your Rock 'n' Roll, they'll still be listening to the big bands.'

Linda was delighted with her new image. 'I'm a different person,' she said with delight as she looked again at herself in the mirror. Her auburn hair, cut in waves down to her shoulders, now had a sheen about it. Sally had also plucked her eyebrows and darkened them with a pencil. The merest hint of eyeshadow had so enhanced her brown eyes, they now appeared to shine. A slightly darker shade of lipstick made her mouth rounder and fuller.

'I didn't feel much like going out earlier,' Linda said, her voice lifted, 'but I do now.'

'Tell you what, then,' Sally responded. 'Let's take a walk to the Greyhound and have a couple of drinks. I'll leave a note for my fella and tell him to catch up with us there.'

Linda looked at Sally in appreciation. 'Only if you're sure. I don't want you and Steve falling out over me.'

'Don't be daft. He'll be having a drink after the match. It'll give him a good excuse to go straight back out again. Give me a knock at seven.'

Sally left and Linda went to her bedroom wardrobe. She picked out a pink and white candy striped dress with a full skirt and a plunging neckline. With it she would wear a broad white belt which she knew accentuated her slim waist-line and full breasts. The final touch was to be a pair of pink stiletto high heels.

Tonight she would dress to kill.

42

7pm

An hour later, Linda draped a pink angora
sweater over her shoulders and took a final look in
the mirror. She found it difficult to believe she
was looking at her own reflection. 'You can take
your pick tonight, Linda Watson,' she said
smiling.

Sally, dressed in a tight, white pencil-slim skirt
and elevated on four-inch stiletto heels, whistled
approval at her friend's new look. 'How have you
managed to hide such beauty for so long?' she
asked.

'Just a knack I've had,' Linda replied. 'You
don't look too bad yourself.'

Indeed, Sally too was dressed to turn heads.
Her skirt was complimented with a white blouse
and a red bow tie and over her arm she carried a
white bolero jacket. Her heels forced her to kick a
shapely leg out sideways and her hair bobbed as
she took Linda's arm. The two girls made their
way down the path and giggled all the way to the
Greyhound on East Prescot Road.

Billy knotted his blue, polka-dot tie and fitted his
opal tie-stud and matching cuff-links. Slipping on
the jacket of his grey shark-skin suit, he turned to
the mirror and ran a comb through his black,

curly hair. Satisfied with the result, he made his way downstairs.

His Ma, dad, sister Katie and brother Bobby were watching The Perry Como Show and paid him scant attention as he told his Ma not to wait up.

'How come everyone's staying in?' Billy asked.

'Your dad didn't back the winner in the National,' his Ma answered, 'so we can't afford to go out.'

'I thought you'd have backed it, Ma,' Billy said, smiling. 'The kitchen's always stocked with Oxo cubes.'

'Yes, I know. I could have kicked myself when it won. I backed The Crofter. Fell at Becher's.'

'What did you back, Dad.'

'Flippin' Wyndburgh. Ten-to-one second. If Tim Brookshaw hadn't lost his irons going over Becher's, he'd have won by the length of our street.'

Billy shook his head. 'That's hard luck, Dad. Didn't you back the second last year?'

'Tiberetta, thirty-three-to-one.'

'And the year before?'

'Wyndburgh again. Twenty-five-to-one.'

'You'll have to see the doctor, Dad. That's as bad a case of seconditis as I've ever heard of.'

'Don't remind me.'

Billy laughed and left them to their evening with the television. They would watch The Army Game and Wagon Train and later on The Arthur Haynes Show. Billy was not a big fan of television, but it seemed that now more and more people were watching television.

He left the house and walked up King's Avenue and was about to cross East Prescot Road and make for the Knotty Ash when he changed his mind and decided to first call into the Greyhound.

Linda and Sally were seated in the corner of the buffet bar, each drinking pale ale and lime. The bar was beginning to fill with couples out for the evening. A group of teenagers were at the bar, preparing to leave for the Knotty Ash village hall to see the local beat group, Rory Storm and the Hurricanes.

'Fancy coming for a dance, girls?' one of the group called over to Linda and sally.

'No, thanks,' Sally called back. 'We're waiting for someone.'

Another of the lads, having drunk enough to have sufficient Dutch-courage, walked over to them. He looked smart in his Italian three-button suit and his hair was combed forward in the Tony Curtis style. He placed his hands on their table and leaned towards them. 'Come on, girls. Me and my mate, Johno, will show you a good time.'

Sally looked him straight in the eye. 'Isn't it a bit past your bedtime?

The other lads laughed and the young man sheepishly backed away. Within a minute, the group left.

'Don't know what your missing,' the wounded flirt called over his shoulder.

Sally blew him a kiss and smiled sweetly.

'He wasn't a bad-looking lad,' Linda said.

'But too young,' Sally added. 'We'd have been accused of cradle-snatching.'

'Ready for another?' Linda asked.

'A vodka and orange this time,' Sally replied. 'Two pale ales are more than enough for me.'

Linda stood at the bar and ordered two vodkas.

'Everything all right, miss?' Ritchie, the barman, asked.

'All right?' Linda asked in response.

'Those lads. They didn't cause you any problems?'

'Oh no. They're just out for a bit of fun.' As she took her change and picked up the two glasses, the buffet door opened and in walked Billy. This, she thought, could be more trouble than a bunch of young lads.

He recognised her immediately, but knew this was a very different Linda to the one he had known for the past three months. Very different, indeed.

Limping on his stick, he made his way to the bar as Linda, ignoring him, returned to her seat.

'You look like you've just seen a ghost,' Sally said.

'No ghost. Look who's standing at the bar.'

'Oh, my God,' Sally gasped. 'Of all the people.'

Linda was seated with her back to Billy and said to Sally, 'I hope he takes the hint, but it's not likely. He'll be over in a minute.'

Billy ordered a highball from Ritchie, a man he

had known since he was kid.

'Have they been here long?' he asked, nodding towards the girls without looking at them.

'About an hour,' Ritchie answered.

'What are they drinking?'

'They've just gone onto vodka and orange.'

'On their own?'

'Yeah. A couple of likely lads tried to chat them up, but they chased them.'

Billy nodded. 'No boyfriends, then?'

'No boyfriends. Which one do you fancy?'

'The redhead. I've been out with her a few times, but I've been seeing the barmaid in the Red House. To be honest, Ritchie, the barmaid's a bit of a nutcase, and if I had my way I'd like to get back with Linda over there.' He pulled a pound note from his pocket. 'Give me another highball, Ritchie, and two vodkas and orange.'

Ritchie smiled. 'Fools rush in where angels fear to tread.'

Billy picked up the drinks and walked over to the table, placing them before the two girls.

Linda spoke without acknowledging Billy's presence. 'I don't remember ordering more drinks, Sal. Do you?'

Sally, feeling the tension, did not reply.

'Ah, come on, Lin,' Billy cut in with his broadest smile. 'Call it a peace offering. I know I'm not the most reliable person in the world, but I don't do it on purpose.'

Linda ignored him and again spoke to Sally. 'I wonder who he spent the night with last night,

Sal. But wherever he was, I bet you he'll have a beauty for an excuse. He always does.'

'I think I'll go and powder my nose,' Sally said, more than a little embarrassed by the scene being played out before her.

'You stay where you are, Sal,' Linda said quickly. 'Somebody else is leaving.'

'Look, Lin,' Billy spluttered. 'I got caught up with a couple of mates I used to sail with. I haven't seen them for ages.'

'Well, I hope you'll all be very happy together.'

'No, seriously,' Billy persisted. 'When they heard about what I've been through recently, they insisted on making a fuss of me. We went into the Baltic Fleet on the other side of town. It started out as a quick couple of pints and before I knew it – '

'Tell it to the marines,' Linda cut in.

'It's true, Lin. I ended up rat-faced in the Seven Stars and kipped on a mates couch in Park Road.'

'One of your better stories, Billy Walsh,' Linda said, but Billy could tell her attitude was softening.

'I love you, Lin,' Billy said with feeling, thinking he was nearly there.

Sally, more embarrassed than ever, was about to get up and leave them to it for a minute, when Her boyfriend Steve walked in. She waved to him with relief and he joined them.

Once he had a drink, Steve sat down.

This is perfect, Billy thought. She can hardly be rude to me now.

Indeed, Linda put away the sarcasm and for the next hour Billy was able to use his charms. When Steve and Sally declared it was time to go, Billy offered to walk Linda home.

'Haven't you got somewhere to go?' Linda asked a little tersely.

'Only the Knotty Ash,' Billy replied. 'I'm meeting Vic, but you can join us if you like.'

'Not tonight, Billy. I need a little time to think things through.'

'Tomorrow then?'

Linda didn't answer. Instead, she picked up her cardigan and followed Steve and Linda outside. When they reached the house, Steve and sally said goodnight and went inside.

Billy immediately took Linda's hand and pulled her close, kissing her lightly on the lips. He did not expect her to respond, but she put an arm around his neck and parting her lips, kissed him long and hard.

When they broke, she rested her head on his chest.

'If I pick you up at seven,' Billy suggested, 'we could go to the Tower Ballroom and dance to,Bill Gregson and his Orchestra.'

'You can't dance anymore, Billy.'

'A slow waltz with you is like a fast tango with Miss World.'

'Oh, very smooth, Billy Walsh, but okay. It's a date. But if you let me down again, I won't ever speak to you again.'

'I've learnt my lesson.'

43

9.10pm

Carol looked at the clock high on the wall of the bar. He's cutting it fine, she thought. If he doesn't turn up, I'll kill him.

One of the regulars was playing a concertina, accompanied by old Charlie on the spoons. Agnes, seventy if she was a day, was killing On Mother Kelly's Doorstep, but her efforts were appreciated by those assembled around her. When she finished, she was greeted with enthusiastic applause.

'Come on, Ernie,' a voice shouted. 'Give us a song.'

'Oh, God,' Carol murmured. 'Here we go. Old Swan's answer to Al Jolsen!'

Ernie needed no second bidding. He stood up, took a mouthful of dark rum and broke into an old Jolsen number: Where Did Robinson Crusoe Go With Friday on Saturday Night?

'Give us a pint of mild, Queen,' a red-nosed drunk slurred. He'd been knocking them back since opening time and showed no inclination to stop.

'Haven't you got a wife to go home to?' Carol asked.

'Probably,' he answered with indifference.

Carol shook her head and began pulling his

pint just as Billy strode into the bar.

'You're here, then.'

'Aye,' Billy answered and ordered a highball.

'I can get straight off at ten. Betty said she'd cover for me. And guess what.'

'What?'

'She said she'll stand in for me tomorrow night so we can spend all Sunday together.'

'Oh, really,' Billy said. Oh, shit, he thought. 'That's great.'

'We could go and see Beryl Bryden and the Alex Welsh band at the Cavern. What do you think?'

'I'll leave it up to you,' was all he could think of to say. Only God knew how he was going to straighten this out. He dared not let Linda down again.

The Cavern was not Billy's scene. Hot, moist and foul-smelling, he always felt over-dressed on the few occasions he went there. Most of the men there wore corduroy trousers and woollen sweaters. Never a shirt and tie in sight. But it was, as Carol was quick to point out, the 'in-place' for the city's beatniks.

Billy thought the music was okay. Alex Welsh had a good, tight band and they played New Orleans jazz. But he would have been happier listening to it in a more comfortable environment.

They had been there for an hour when Billy tapped Carol on the shoulder and pointed to the stairs. Back in Matthew Street, Billy visibly sighed with relief. 'How do people put up with that all night?'

'It's the music, but if you think it was packed tonight, you should go when one of the new beat grouped is playing.'

They began walking towards Church Street.

'What's a beat group?' Billy asked.

'It's the new sound. Three or four guitars and drums. The kids are going crazy about it.'

'Where do they play?'

'Oh, all over the place. Hope Hall in Hope Street, the Blue Ball -'

'The Blue Ball?'

'Yeah. Pretty soon they'll be playing it wherever you go. It attracts the kids, so there's always a lot of fighting, but the music's great.'

By this time, they were walking up Bold Street, making for the Havana Club.

'Are you sure we can get in here?' Billy asked. 'I've heard you need a letter from the Pope to get past the bouncers.'

'Yeah, we'll be okay. A fella I know called Eddie works on the door. He lives on Queens Drive and drinks in the Red House. He's told me to come down a hundred times. Just slip him ten bob.'

'What's it like?'

'Dancing on the second floor, gambling on the first floor and food on the ground floor. It's nice. You'll like it.'

At the top of Bold street, they turned left into Berry Street and approached the club. They met

Eddie on the door and, after Billy had slipped him a ten shilling note, asked them to sign the visitors' book.

They made their way to the second floor and Billy was pleasantly surprised to find a well-appointed lounge with plush seats and a small dance floor. In one corner was a stage on which was a piano, drums, bass and saxophone quartet playing, led by Mitch Morris.

They found a seat near the bar and ordered their drinks. The group were playing The Girl From Ipenema and Billy immediately thought this was more like it. This place will still be going, he considered, when the Cavern was dead and buried.

Mitch Morris thanked the audience for their polite applause and introduced the next number, Call me Irresponsible. Billy thought he was a decent singer and he liked the laid-back style of the saxophonist. He watched as two older women on the next table, in their mid-thirties, tapped their feet to the rhythm of the music.

He ordered another highball for himself and sherry for Carol. As he paid for the drinks, one of the older women caught Billy's eye and raised her glass. Billy nodded in response and then returned his attention to Carol.

Throughout the next hour, each time Billy glanced across at the woman she was staring at him, smiling at him seductively. Her skin was pale against the contrast of her brunette hair and black dress. Her high cheek bones gave her a sensuous air and Billy felt strongly attracted to her.

Jesus, he thought, under different circumstances, I'd be on here.

At that moment, Carol stood up. 'I'm just off to powder my nose. Won't be a minute.'

As she disappeared, Mitch Morris announced the next number. 'This is a fox-trot, ladies and gentlemen. So let's see some of you on the floor as we play for you Dancing in the dark.'

This was a particular favourite of Billy's, especially the Frank Sinatra version. He heard it the first time in New York a year earlier, backed by the Billy May orchestra. His attention was so much drawn to the way this quartet handled the number, he did not notice the slim figure glide alongside him until she spoke.

'Didn't you hear the man? He wants people to dance.'

Billy turned to see the dark-haired woman looking directly into his eyes.

'I'm sorry,' Billy answered quickly, glancing across towards the Ladies toilet to see if Carol was on her way back. She wasn't. 'I'm not fit for dancing.'

'Oh, you disappoint me,' she answered smoothly. 'Can't you manage a very slow fox-trot?'

Billy had an unobstructed view of her cleavage and found it difficult to speak. This woman is hot, he thought. 'Doctor's orders,' he croaked. 'No dancing until further notice.'

'Well, as soon as you get the all clear, you come running back here. I want the first dance.'

'I see the doctor Thursday. If he says I can dance, I might just make my here . . . if it's worth my while.'

The woman reached across the table and picked up a book of complimentary matches from the Scafell Hotel in Lord Nelson Street. Billy had never heard of it, but there must have been two dozen small bed and breakfast hotels up there, around the corner from Lime Street Station. Flipping open the packet, she took a pen from her handbag and wrote inside: Royal 7714 - Lola.

'I'm here most weekends, but why don't you ring me on Thursday just to make sure.' She looked at him provocatively. 'It will be worth your while.'

Billy read the message. 'Is it true what they say? Lola gets what Lola wants.

She ran a finger under his chin and leaned forward to whisper in his ear. 'Always.'

As she left to return to her friend, Billy slumped back in his seat and, closing his eyes, exhaled slowly. As he opened them, he was confronted by an agitated Carol standing in front of him.

'What did she want?'

'What did who want?'

'Don't play the little innocent, Billy. That one there. I saw her leaving the table as I came back in. What did she want?'

'Oh, her. Nothing. She thought I was someone else.'

'I bet she did.' Carol placed her hands on her hips. 'Are you shooting me a line?'

'Keep your hair on and sit down.'

Carol was not easily appeased. 'If you're messing me about, Billy, you'll regret it.'

Billy let out a sigh of exasperation. 'You saw her leaving the table, yes? She went away. Doesn't that tell you something? You didn't see me at her table. She was here and she went away. Okay?'

Billy ordered more drinks and put his arm around Carol. She quickly softened.

Mitch Morris was back on the microphone. 'Now ladies and gentlemen, the moment you have been waiting for, especially, dare I say it, the gentlemen in the room. Once again, I am proud to introduce to you the sexy, no, erotic, sensational Miss Lola Lovelady!'

As Billy's jaw dropped, Carol shook her head. 'Oh, that's just great! The gorgous Lola Lovethingy has just mistaken you for someone else. Who? Tony flippin' Bennett?' She stood up and announced, 'I'm off!'

Billy grabbed her arm. 'Don't be daft. Sit down.'

In response, Carol dug her fingernails into the back of Billy's hand until she drew blood. Once he released her arm, she walked out.

Billy had nearly cried out, but Lola had started singing Cry Me a River and he stifled the pain. He chased after Carol, but she was back in Berry Street before he caught up with her.

'Jesus, Carol! Talk about over-reacting.'

'Don't take me for a fool, Billy. Next time it'll be your looks that suffer!'

'This is over the top.'

'Then don't give me any more of your bullshit! If you think you can hop from my bed into someone else's, then think again.'

'It's you I want. Why do you think I chased after you?'

As suddenly as she had snapped, Carol's anger subsided. 'If you want me, show it,' she said softly, putting her arms around him. She kissed him passionately. 'I need some of that loving we had last night. Flag a cab and let's get home.'

Relieved, Billy hailed a passing taxi, but as they climbed in he could not help thinking he would be back in the Havana Club before long in different company.

Once they were back in the flat, Carol wanted Billy between the sheets as quickly as she could move him, almost ripping the shirt off his back. It seemed to Billy she was a woman of extremes and he had no doubts which extreme he preferred. On this occasion, her passion was almost too much for him. She bit and scratched him and by the time they were done, Billy lay breathless and wounded.

'I'm sorry about being so angry earlier,' she said softly, her appetite finally sated. 'But I'll make it up to you all over again tomorrow.'

Oh, Christ, Billy thought, I've got to get out of this, but how? The bitch will kick-off all over again. 'I've arranged to meet a few mates tomorrow,' he offered finally.

'Well, cancel it,' Carol responded abruptly.

'I can't. I need to get back to work as soon as I can and the lads can put me straight on how to get past the medical on Thursday. They sail next Monday, so it's the only chance I've got to see them.'

'Where are you meeting them?' she asked firmly. 'Maybe you can bring them to the Red House. I might as well go to work if I'm not seeing you.'

'I'm meeting them in the Knotty Ash, but then we're going down to the Dingle. That's where most of the lads live.'

'All right,' she said, 'I'll let you off this time, but don't make any plans for the next few days. From now on, you're mine.'

44

Sunday
8.30pm

'Must go,' Billy said. 'I've got a hundred things to do.'

'Leave me some cigarettes,' Carol said, sleepily.

Billy took one and threw her the packet. 'I'll get some on the way home,' he said.

Carol propped herself up on one elbow. 'Be a love,' she said, reaching for the cigarettes, 'and put the kettle on.'

Billy looked for his jacket and found it on the floor behind the chair, where Carol had dragged it off him the night before. He pulled his lighter from his jacket pocket and lit the gas ring. 'See you,' he called out, and quickly made for the door. Had he not been in such a hurry, he might have noticed the book of matches that dropped from his jacket to the floor.

Once he was home, Billy went straight to bed and stayed there until he was woken by the smell of his mother's cooking. Roast lamb. That smell could make a dead man hungry, Billy thought.

As he dressed, he thought about the events of the previous night. Even by his own standards, it was a rare night: making up with Carol, meeting Lola and spending the night with Carol. Carol, he decided, would have to go. Too dangerous, too short a fuse. Linda, yes. He looked forward to being back with Linda. She was a girl he could get serious about. But not before he had sampled Lola's wares.

'You awake?' his mother shouted up the stairs.

'Yes, Ma,' he called back.

'It's twelve o'clock. You're supposed to be meeting Vic in the Knotty Ash in quarter-of-an-hour.'

'Oh, shit!' Billy said, forgetting himself.

'What was that?'

'Nothing. I'll be down in a minute.'

Carol made a half-hearted attempt to tidy up, but she did not get far. Picking up a cup that lay empty on its side by the armchair, her attention was drawn to what looked like a small piece of card. Picking it up, she saw it was a book of matches.

Twenty minutes later, she was at her father's door.

Jimmy was surprised to see his daughter. She never called around on a Sunday, so something was wrong. Boyfriend trouble, he decided. He turned off the television and turned towards her. 'Come on, then. What's the problem?'

'That bloody Billy Walsh! That's the problem!'

'Is it the same family I was thinking of?'

'Yes. He lives in Kings Avenue. His dad's name is Jack and he used to be a docker.'

Jimmy nodded. 'I could have saved you a lot of heartache there, love. The family's no good.'

'How do you know Billy's dad,' Carol asked. 'You never told me.'

Jimmy took a deep breath. 'I've never told you how I damaged my hand. To be honest, I don't like talking about it. But if you've got your heart set on this Walsh lad, there's a few things you should know about his father.'

'His dad had something to do with you accident?' Carol asked, intrigued.

'More than something. We were loading pallets of whisky into the ship's hold and Jack Walsh was on the guide rope. We were told to stop because of a hold-up further along the line. Anyway, Jack takes a turn around a cleat and after a few minutes, the hold-up is cleared and we're told to carry on. The next thing I know, this pallet is flying towards me after that bastard Walsh pushed it towards me. I tried to jump clear of it, but it caught my left hand and crushed it against the bulkhead.'

Carol was shocked. 'So what happened to Billy's dad? Wasn't he prosecuted?'

'He should have been, but he wasn't. There was an inquiry. He said the rain increased the tension on the holding rope. When he took a turn off the cleat, the rope was yanked from his hands and although he tried to stop it, he couldn't. He even had the gall to say he put his back out trying to stop the pallet. He was on the sick for weeks.'

'So that was it? Nothing else happened?'

'It was his word against mine and I couldn't prove anything. The inquiry decided it was an accident. The best part was I had to fight them tooth and bloody nail to get my compensation. Jack bloody Walsh was pensioned off and looked after.'

'Why would he do such a thing to you, Dad?'

'We never liked each other. He was an agitator. They called themselves Socialists, but that's just another word for a bloody Commy! He used to have us walking off the dock for the least little thing. I tell you, for every penny we won through going on strike, we lost two because of it. I used to vote against strike every time, and it peeved him because I wouldn't be intimidated. It came to a head when he called for a stoppage over 'clean-up' time. We were loading oil drums and Jack Walsh wanted us to be paid an extra half-an-hour's money for the time it took us to get cleaned up. The boss said we could have the half-hour off, but we wouldn't get paid for it. He offered to pay us for ten minutes.

'Jack said "no deal" and called a stoppage, but me and a couple of other lads argued against it. We won the day and we went back to work. At the end of the day, when everyone else was gone, he waited for me in the wash room and told me to be careful. He threatened me. Said if I kept getting in his way, he'd have me sorted out. We exchanged a few words and the next thing I know is he hits me on the side of the head. Before I could collect me wits, he was all over me. He got the better of me for a minute, but then I managed to catch him with a straight right on the nose.

After that it was an even fight and we knocked seven bells out of each other. There was blood everywhere. In the end we were both exhausted. I picked meself and started going home, but as I did he shouted after me. "I'll have you, Roberts," he said. "Mark my words, I'll have you." And he did.'

Carol could not believe the coincidence. 'First the father messes with you and now the son's messing with me. It looks to me likes it time to put the record straight with these Walshes.'

Jimmy shook his head. 'Best forget it, love. It's not worth the hassle.'

'Oh, it'll be worth it all right. I'll make sure it's worth it.'

Billy and Vic found a quiet corner in the lounge of the Knotty Ash Hotel and Billy brought Vic up to date.

'You're cracked, mate,' Vic told him. 'You've got two strung along and now you're working on a third. How are going to keep it up?'

'Oh, I'll manage. Anyway, you should see this Lola one. She's just too classy to pass by, Vic. You'd think the same if you saw her.'

'Maybe, Billy, but I've been going steady with Marie since we met up at your house in January. We're thinking of getting engaged in the summer.'

'Oh, well, each to his own.' Billy emptied his glass and stood up to go to the bar. 'Couldn't do me a favour, could you, Vic?'

'It's not a favour you need, Billy. It's a bloody manager.'

Billy laughed. 'You could be right, but I need the loan of a car.'

'What for?'

'Well, I'm seeing Linda tonight and it might be a good idea to keep clear of the beaten track. You don't know who might see me. One wrong word in the wrong place and all that.'

'For once, you're right. Be here at seven. I'll have something lined up for you.'

That night, Billy called for Linda just before seven and they made their way to the Knotty Ash to meet Vic. Vic was at the bar waiting for them. The pub had been opened only a matter of minutes and there were only two other customers in.

Vic handed Billy a set of keys as he got the drinks in. 'It's a white Austin Cambridge,' he said. 'Column change, bench seat in the front. You'll find it parked out front.'

'You're a real pal, Vic. I'm taking Linda over the water to New Brighton.'

'Yeah, you should be safe enough over there,' Vic said smiling.

Billy stole him a glance as Linda's ears picked up.

'Safe?' she asked.

Vic coughed. 'Er, yeah. Should be. You know, the roads are nice and quiet over there.'

'Take no notice of him,' Billy said. 'He likes to

think he's the only person round here who knows how to drive a car.'

'Don't worry, Vic,' Linda said, 'I'll make sure he goes slow.'

Vic opened his mouth to give the obvious response, but a swift kick under the table from Billy stopped him.

'We won't hang around Vic,' Billy then said. 'But thanks again.' He then took Linda by the arm and made for the door. 'See you.'

'Yeah, have a good night.'

As they walked to the door, Billy took a cigarette and fished around for his lighter. It was then that Carol appeared before them. Billy took a step backward as if hit in the chest with a sledgehammer.

'Need a light?' Carol asked him and offered him the book of matches.

'Carol,' he gasped. 'This is not what it seems.'

Vic watched in amazement. He saw Linda's eyes filling with tears, but the other one was a long way from crying. He decided to get hold of her and pin her arms down, but as he stepped forward, Carol saw him.

'Keep out of it,' she hissed. 'This has got nothing to do with you.'

Momentarily, Vic hesitated and as he did, Carol launched herself at Billy. She took his hair into the fingers of her left hand and raked the fingernails of her right down Billy's cheek. The two of them fell to the floor.

Linda stood transfixed, but she was drawn to

the book of matches the girl had waved in Billy's face and were now on the floor at her feet. She picked them up.

Carol by this time was in a frenzy. She was clawing at his hair and punching wildly at his face.

As Billy tried to protect himself and get to his feet, he pleaded with Carol to stop. She did not listen.

For Christ's sake, Vic,' he shouted finally, 'do something.'

Vic tried to wrestle her to one side, but he couldn't keep hold of her. He did, though, give Billy the opportunity to break free.

Seeing his chance, Billy jumped to his feet and swung his right fist into Carol's nose.

She fell back and though still conscious stopped moving.

Billy looked down at her. 'That's enough,' he said panting. He thought he had been able to extinguish Carol's fire, but as he turned to speak to Linda, Carol leaped at him, driving the heel of her stiletto shoe into the back of Billy's hand. Billy felt himself go sick as the shoe embedded itself into the bone.

This time, Vic took no chances and grabbed Carol by the neck from behind. For a moment, she struggled against his grip, but finally conceded she could not free herself. She stood motionless panting, but Vic would not let her go.

Billy pulled the shoe from his hand and hurled it to the floor. 'Shit!' he called out as the blood spurt out all over his jacket and shirt. 'Shit!' When he turned to talk to Linda, she was already gone.

Now that the fighting was finished, Eugene, the manager appeared.

'Okay, young lady. Either you leave of your own accord or I'll have the police here in two minutes.'

Carol did not even hear him. 'This is not over yet, Billy Walsh,' she snarled, still in Vic's vice-like grip. 'You'll rue the day you ever set eyes on me.'

Eugene stepped forward. 'I said it's time to leave.'

'Don't worry, mate. I'm done for now. If you can get this fuckin' gorilla to let go of my neck, I'll leave you and your shitty pub to your shitty little customers.'

Vic thought that Eugene had never before heard such bad language from a woman and, it was true, he was struck speechless. Vic eased his grip, but was careful to stand between Carol and Billy.

Carol made for the door, but not before she pointed a finger at Billy and barked, 'You and your father are gettin' what's been comin' for a long time.'

Seconds later, she was gone.

A number of people had entered the pub while the attack was taking place, including Ada Molloy. She was delighted by what she had seen.

As the noise of the disturbance abated, conversation sparked off among the regulars. 'To think,' Ada said laughing, 'I nearly stayed in to watch Dicky Valentine on Sunday Night at the London Palladium!' She spoke loud enough to ensure Billy heard every word.

'I need to go after Linda,' Billy said as he tried to stem the blood gushing from his hand.

'No you don't, Billy,' Vic told him. 'Not unless you want a set of scratches down the other cheek. You leave her be.' Vic picked up a bar towel and bound it around Billy's hand. He took another towel and after asking one of the barmaids to dampen it, began to clean up Billy's face. 'It's either home or hospital for you. Where do you want to go? I'll drive you.'

'Home, Vic, but I'll walk. I need some fresh air.'

Billy left the pub with the towel still wrapped around his hand. Making sure carol was not lying in wait for him, he made his way past the post office and the shops towards the Greyhound. He crossed Blackmoor Drive and carried on towards Liverpool City Rugby club. His hand was beginning to throb, but he was feeling a little better when he heard footsteps coming up behind him. He spun around but could see nothing.

He turned into his road and passed Ada Molloy's house. Inside the television was on and he could hear Dicky Valentine singing The Finger of Suspicion. He turned into the path of number twenty-two and, turning the key, went inside.

As the door closed behind him, a figure emerged from behind the gate of the house opposite. Carol stood up straight and touched her bloodied nose and bruised cheek. 'Now I know where you live, Billy Walsh,' she said quietly, 'I'll make your life hell.'

45

Monday
6am

'Mr Walsh?'

The physiotherapist, a large, heavy-set woman in her forties called Billy's name from the door of the treatment room. As he stood and walked towards her, she noticed the scratches on his cheek. 'What happened to your face, young man?' she asked.

'I broke up a fight between two women, Mrs Wilmott,' he replied, entering the room and sitting on the bed. 'This is what I got for my trouble.'

'And the hand?'

'The same.' He took off his socks and shoes and sat on the bed positioned along the far wall.

Mrs Wilmott firmly but gently began to manip-ulate his right ankle, the most badly damaged, but Billy felt no reaction. The left too was free of pain. 'Very good, Mr Walsh. You've been doing your daily exercises.'

'Religiously,' Bill said with a smile.

'Well, I don't think there's anything more I can do for you. I'm happy to discharge you from further treatment. Continue to take it easy, but you should find you can manage without a stick now.'

'What about dancing?' Billy asked.

'In moderation, yes,' she replied. 'But not to excess. There is every chance you will suffer from arthritis in later years, but if you push the joints too hard it will come sooner and be all the more painful. Moderation is the key word, Mr Walsh.'

As Billy put back on his socks and shoes, the physiotherapist looked again at his face. 'I'll have that cleaned up before you go. It could turn septic.'

Billy tried to protest, but to no avail. She left him for a few moments and when she returned he could hear she was in the company of another member of staff.

'Here he is, nurse. His face has been badly scratched and needs to be bathed with an antiseptic wash.'

Billy turned casually towards the pair and was stunned to be confronted by Linda. Before he could splutter one word, she picked up a stainless steel basin and threw the contents across his face.

'Consider your face washed, you lying bastard!' she screamed at him and raised the basin to bring it down on his head.

Billy leaped to one side and the basin crashed onto the bed and bounced across the room.

'Nurse!' Mrs Wilmott cried. 'In God's name, have you gone mad?' She stepped between the pair and turned on Linda. 'I don't know what this is all about, but your conduct is reprehensible whatever the circumstances. Get out and go to Sister Johnson's office. Stay there until I join you.'

Linda began to sob and ran from the room.

Instinctively, Billy knew he would not see her again. He got to his feet and took the towel Mrs Wilmott passed to him.

'Would you like to offer me some form of an explanation, Mr Walsh?' she asked him. 'I can assure you Nurse Watson will in very serious trouble over this incident.'

'Please don't discipline her,' Billy urged. 'If you were aware of the full facts, you would think Linda . . . Nurse Watson, acted with great restraint. I am the villain of the peace here.'

'You will not be making a complaint then?'

'Oh, absolutely not.'

'Very well, then, Mr Walsh. I will speak up on her behalf when I see the sister. I bid you good day.'

Carol's left eye was swollen and was turning a deep purple. The skin on her nose was split and her top lip swollen. On her way to her father's, she stopped at a telephone box and rang the pub to say she would not be in for a few days.

When Jimmy opened the front door, he gasped when he saw the state of Jimmy's face. 'Jesus Christ! What happened to you.'

Carol walked straight past him into the house and made for the kitchen. 'I need a cup of tea,' she said.

Jimmy followed. 'What happened? Who did that to you? '

Carol lit a cigarette and looked her father straight in the eye. 'Billy Walsh.'

'What?' Jimmy could not believe it. 'Christ, I knew the Walshes were no good, but I didn't think they beat women up.'

'Make a cup of tea, Dad, and I'll tell you about it. But it's not over. I know where the bastard lives and I'm going over there today.'

Jimmy stood up. 'Aye, and I'm coming with you.'

Billy arrived at the union office on Mann Island just after one o'clock. In his years at sea he had managed to save more than £700, but over the past three months that had been depleted by nearly £300. The union gave him three pounds and seven shillings sick pay, which meant he would not have to go to the bank that day. With a bit of luck, he would be back at work soon and saving again.

He had decided to call Lola and at two o'clock he went to the telephone box at the top of James Street and called what he hoped was her number. The phone rang just twice before it was answered.

'Royal seven seven one four.'

'Lola?'

'Speaking.'

Thank God, he thought. 'It's me. Billy.'

'Billy who?' she asked.

'We met in the Havana club the other night. You gave me your number.'

'Oh, the man who couldn't dance. I thought you were ringing me on Thursday.'

Billy had worked this out. 'Yeah, well, if I'm

passed fit for work I might be sailing on Thursday.'

'Sailing?' Lola asked.

'Yeah. I'm in the merch. I might not be able to see you after tomorrow, so I thought -'

'You thought I might be available today. Where are you?'

'Queens Square. By the Victoria Monument.'

'Okay. Jump a bus to Hardman Street. I live in Hope Street. Number thirty-three.'

'Now?' Billy had not been expecting this.

'Why not?'

'No reason. I'll be there in twenty minutes.'

'Bring some milk and a packet of cigarettes with you. Kensitas.'

Billy replaced the handset and punched the air. 'Yes!'

Hope Street was on the edge of the city centre and he could have walked the distance in fifteen minutes, but instead he took Lola's advice and caught a bus. Little more than ten minutes later he was ringing the bell on the door of number thirty-three, a pint of milk and packet of twenty Kensitas in his hand.

The house was a three-storey Victorian end terrace in a street that was Liverpool's equivalent of Harley Street, with many of the houses being used by solicitors, architects and private doctors.

When Lola opened the door, he was surprised, but hardly disappointed, to see her still wearing her night-dress under a dressing gown hanging loosely open.

'You look like you've just seen a ghost,' she said, knowing very well her ample charms were the cause of Billy's distraction.

'It's not every day I'm greeted by such a vision of beauty,' he responded, smiling.

'Sorry I'm not dressed,' she said demurely, returning his smile. 'I was working late last night. I'd only just got up when you rang.'

'Absolutely no need to apologise.'

He followed her into the house and they entered the sitting room. The highly polished floor was covered with Chinese rugs and on either side of the room there were two enormous, leather Chesterfield couches. A large circular glass coffee table sat between them and in the bay window was a grand piano.

Billy looked about him and whistled.

'I'm impressed,' he said finally.

'Oh, none of it's mine. I rent the place. The furniture was already here.'

'Must cost a few bob.'

'It's not cheap.' She took the milk and cigarettes of Billy and opened the packet straight away. Lighting up, she sat down and crossed her legs, making no attempt to cover up.

'So you're a merchant seaman, Billy,' she said, looking at him seductively. 'You must get about.'

'New York and Montreal mostly, but I've been to most places over the years.'

'A girl friend in every port?'

Billy laughed. 'There's not as much time for that as people like to think.'

'And what about the girl you were with in the Havana Club?'

'That's finished.'

'Is she the one responsible for the scratches and the bandaged hand.'

'Yeah, she didn't take it too well.'

Lola threw her head back as she laughed. 'You're not kidding!' She stood up and walked across to the drinks cabinet. 'Let's forget the coffee,' she said. 'Do you fancy a scotch.'

'Why not?' Bill replied and a moment later Lola handed him a generous glassful of Bell's twelve-year-old. She then sat at the piano and began to play. As Billy turned to listen, she started singing.

'Holding hands at midnight,

'Neath the starry sky,

Nice work, if you can get it,

And you can get it if you try.'

She had a smoky, smouldering voice and her long, slender fingers effortlessly picked out the melody.

Billy was caught like a fly in a spider's web. He walked across towards her and leaned on the piano silently as she continued with the song. When she was finished, she carried on with a tango.

'Whatever Lola wants,

Lola gets,

And little man,

All that Lola wants is you.'

When she was finished, she reached for Billy's tie and pulled him towards her. They kissed passionately. When they finally separated, Billy's head was swimming.

'Do you have a record player,' he managed to say.

She pointed to a radiogram in the corner and Billy switched it on and went through her records. Among them he found an LP by Frankie Laine and the second track, A Woman in Love, was just what he was looking for. He picked up the coffee table and moved to one side of the room and as the song started, he raised his hand to Lola in an invitation to join him in the centre of the room.

'I owe you a dance,' he said.

Lola nodded and moved towards him. The voice of Frankie Laine filled the room, singing, 'Your eyes are the eyes of a woman in love.'

Billy held her close as he moved first one way and then the other, letting her fall into his right arm and then his left. He snapped her sharply upright and then, with his hand in the small of her back, he glided with her across the room. She arched backwards as he placed his right leg between her thighs. As their faces came close again, he could see the excitement in her eyes. After arching again, this time over Billy's left knee, she straightened and he could see her breasts heaving. He then spun with her back across the room and as the song finished, he held her tightly.

She put her fingers through his hair and pulled him forward. As their lips touched, Billy felt a surge of adrenaline flowing through him.

'My God, Billy, you sure can tango.'

'I'll probably regret it later, but that was one dance I had to have.'

She moved to one of the Chesterfields and motioned to Billy to join her. 'You like me, don't you, Billy?' she asked, her eyes sparkling.

'Like you? That's an understatement. I'm bowled over by you.'

They kissed again and Billy put his hand to her breast. She did not resist for several moments, then suddenly she broke away and sat upright.

'Why don't we go out for a drink later? Then we get something to eat and bring it back here.'

Billy, trying to calm himself down, looked at her and smiled. 'Okay. Give me a time and I'll pick you up here?'

'Oh, there's no need to do that. You can spend the afternoon here.' With that, she took Billy by the hand and led him to her bedroom.

46

7pm

Carol entered the Smoke Room of the Greyhound Hotel carrying a black holdall. Her father was at the bar with a half-pint of bitter and a glass of scotch in front of him.

'I hope that's your first,' she said. 'I don't want you with me if you're full of ale.'

'Stop your moaning. I've only just got in here.'

Carol ordered herself a vodka and orange and they moved from the bar to one of the tables close to the door.

'What's in the bag?' Jimmy asked.

'The means to make sure everyone knows what a bastard Billy Walsh is. I've got a tin of white paint and a three inch brush.'

'So you're going to give the Walshes front gate a new coat of paint then.'

'I'll be painting, all right. And everyone will know about Billy Walsh when I'm finished. Just watch my back and wait and see. Come on. Finish your drink.'

As they approached the Walsh household, Carol noticed a lorry parked outside the house next door, its load of sacking covered by a large canvas sheet. She placed the holdall on the floor and took out the tin of paint and brush.

Within a few moments, she was busy daubing

the sheet in white paint. When she was finished, she stepped back to admire her handiwork.

In letters a foot high she had written, 'BILLY WALSH IS A RAPIST!'

'Jesus, Carol, is that true?'

'Of course it's not true. So what?'

'He'll have you in court!'

'Carol smiled. 'Somehow I don't think so.' She went to other side of the lorry and repeated the message.

'Come on,' Jimmy said nervously. 'That's enough. Let's go.'

'Not yet, Dad. I've plenty of paint left.'

Jimmy's raised voice attracted the attention of Ada Molloy, living two doors away, who was adjusting a bedroom curtain. When she reads the words on Vinnie Tillotson's lorry, she gasped.

'My God, what's he been up to now?' she said. There was no love lost between the Molloys and the Walshes, but she knew Billy was no rapist and of late she had been trying to build bridges between the two families. She quickly made her way downstairs and into the street. 'What's going on here?' she shouted

'Mind your own bleedin' business,' Carol snapped back.

'And who are you?' Ada responded, never easily repelled.

Jimmy stepped forward to block her path.

'Don't you dare touch me, you friggin' ape!' She looked over his shoulder and could see no movement from the Walsh house. 'Queenie! Jack!' she screamed.

Jimmy grabbed her by the shoulders and raised a hand to her mouth. 'Be quiet you stupid bitch!'

Ada kicked out and caught him on the shin. As he stumbled back in pain, she rushed forward and pushed him to the floor. As he struggled to his feet, the Walshes' front door opened. It was Jack.

'What the 'ell's goin' on 'ere?' he roared.

Carol helped her father to his feet and urged him to move. 'Come on, Dad. Let's go now, Ignore him.'

At that moment, Jack read the words on Vinnie's lorry and then recognised Jimmy Roberts. 'I'll have you for this, pal!' he roared and made his way down the path.

Jimmy turned to face him. 'You're welcome to try, bud.'

At this point, Vinnie came to his door to see what the fuss was about. When he saw what had been across the canvas sheet, he strode purposefully towards Carol with the paint and brush still in her hand.

'I'll have that, love' he said firmly as he walked towards her.

'You can have it if you want it,' she said and swung the tin at Vinnie's head.

Vinnie ducked and the tin arced harmlessly over his head, but not without first depositing its contents across his back and shoulders.

Jack and Jimmy moved towards each other with menace.

'I've waited a long time for this,' Jimmy said.

'Me and you both,' Jack countered.

Before the two men were close enough to land a blow at each other, Carol stepped between them and swung the paint tin again, this time catching Jack on the side of the head.

As he stumbled, Jimmy saw his chance and struck Jack with a vicious right on the nose. He followed it with a left to his cheek and Jack fell to his knees.

The neighbours were now out watching in numbers and gaped silently at the fight taking place.

Carol screamed at her father. 'Do him, Dad! Do him!'

Jack quickly took stock off his situation and seeing Jimmy momentarily relaxed, launched himself from the ground and seized his assailant around the arms in a vice-like grip. The two men were locked together face-to-face.

'Got you now, you bastard!' Jack hissed. He brought his head back and snapped it forward, butting Jimmy in the face. There was a sickening crack as Jimmy's nose broke. He screamed in agony.

Jack followed this by raising his knee violently into his opponent's groin. When the knee came up for a second time, Jimmy went limp. Jack released the man and allowed him to fall to floor. He then stood over him and bending down hit him twice in the stomach. Jimmy gasped as the breath was driven from his body.

Queenie raised her hands to her face in horror. 'For God's sake someone, stop them.' She then sent Bobby to fetch the police before matters got completely out of hand.

Jack looked to one side to see Carol approaching him once again with the swinging paint tin, but this time Vinnie intervened and grabbed her by the arm. He snatched the tin from her and pushed her heavily into the hedge by the Walshes' gate.

With Jack's attention momentarily distracted, Jimmy was able to crawl away from him and scrambling to his feet, ran off down the road.

Vinnie stood by Jack's side as Carol disentangled herself from the privet hedge and chased after her father.

Billy put his arm around Lola as they cimbed the steps to her front door. They had been out drinking in the Philharmonic pub at the top of Hardman Street and now, just turned eleven o'clock, Lola struggled to place the key in the lock. Finally, the door swung open and they both stumbled into the hallway.

'Steady now,' Billy said quietly.

'Oh, I'm all right,' Lola answered, beginning to giggle.

The idea had been to make some coffee, but as Lola put her arm around Billy's waist and ran her other hand across his groin, any thoughts of going to the kitchen were abandoned.

In the early hours of the morning, they lay exhausted and sated.

Billy lit two cigarettes and passed one to Lola. 'I've never come across anyone like you before,' he said quietly, smiling.

'That goes for me too, Billy,' she said, propping herself on one elbow and gazing deeply into his eyes. 'We should do more together.'

'What do you mean?' Billy asked.

'Well, most of the people I meet are in show-business in one way or another. But you're completely outside of it. It might make things difficult. It's not easy going out with someone who stands on a stage most nights of the week. We're a bit different from everyone else. Not easy to understand.'

'I'm doing okay so far,' Billy suggested.

'That you are,' Lola said with a smile, 'but it would be better if you were involved in my show in some way.'

'How could I do that? I can't sing, can't play anything.'

'I don't know. I suppose you could always . . . ' Lola hesitated.

'What?' Billy prompted her.

'No, nothing. It doesn't matter.'

'Tell me,' Billy insisted.

'Well,' she said finally, 'there's a promoter from Blackpool who's seen me a few times and he thinks he's got just the song for me. One that could launch me into the big-time.'

'How did you meet him?'

'He owns a few small hotels in Liverpool. He has the occasional lounge cabaret show. I was

231

booked to appear at one of them and afterwards we had a chat.'

'What kind of song is it?' Billy asked.

'A love song, like a ballad. The kind of song Julie London might sing. Or Julie Christie or Lena Horne.'

'What's it called?'

'It Hurts When I'm in Love. The promoter said he was thinking of offering it to Alma Cogan, but he says it might be a bit too strong for her. He was on the verge of giving it to Joan Savage or Lita Roza, and then he heard me.'

Billy was impressed with the names she was dropping. 'So where do I come in?'

'Oh, I don't think you do, Billy. It was just a thought best left unsaid.'

'Try me anyway.'

'Well, if I take up the offer of cutting the record, I'll have to go to London for at least three months so I can record the song and promote it.'

'Sounds great, but I still don't see where that might include me.'

'I can't afford to go. I need to stay in the best hotels and eat in the best places. It's all part of the image. I won't make any money until the record starts to sell. I know it's a hit for someone and it's frustrating that money will stop it from being me.'

'What do you need?' Billy asked her.

'I need someone to sponsor me, someone to put up some money. The return on the investment would come from the sales of the record.'

'I meant how much do you need?'

'Oh, about three-hundred pounds.'

Billy let out a low whistle. He had about four hundred pounds left in his depleted savings account.

'See? I told you. It's too much.'

'What about the record companies?' Billy asked.

'The song has to be recorded first and then taken around the different record companies. The promotor does that, but he knows everyone worth knowing at Decca and Pye.'

'Well, don't the record company pay your expenses?'

'Once I'm signed up, yes. But that takes time. I might have to stay in London for three months before I cut a deal.'

Billy nodded. 'So if I invest three hundred pounds in your song, what do I get back?'

'It depends. If it's a hit, you'll make a small fortune. If it does okay, you'll show a handsome profit. Even if it doesn't do well, it will sell enough for you to get your money back. It's a pretty safe bet.'

'Right,' Billy said, deciding to take the plunge. 'I'll go to the bank tomorrow.'

'Oh, Billy,' Lola gasped. 'I don't know what to say.'

Billy grinned. 'You don't have to say anything.'

48

Tuesday
1pm

It was lunch time when Billy walked out of the Midland Bank in Old Swan with three hundred pounds in his wallet. He had mixed emotions about the deal. On the one hand he was elated to be making an investment in a talent like Lola, but he had withdrawn most of what remained of his savings with some trepidation.

He jumped on a number ten bus and a few minutes later was walking down Kings Avenue. He saw Vinnie's lorry and wondered why he wasn't at work. He then saw Vinnie talking to a police officer.

'Everything all right?' Billy called out. At that moment he saw what had been painted on the canvas sheets. 'Shit!'

'No, Billy,' Vinnie said. 'Everything's not all right.'

The police officer looked at Billy. 'Mr Walsh?'

'Yeah, that's me. When did this happen?'

'Last night, Billy,' Vinnie answered. 'There was a right do. The mad woman responsible for this smacked your dad over the head with a paint tin.'

Billy looked up, concern in his eyes. 'Is he okay?'

'Yeah. He's wearing a bloody great turban and he's got a kingsize headache, but he'll live.'

Billy asked Vinnie to describe the woman and he knew immediately who the culprit was. 'Christ, I knew she was a bit mad, but this . . . '

The PC intervened. 'You know who is responsible for this, sir?' he asked.

Billy glanced up at Vinnie, whose facial expression indicated he should say nothing.'

'No. I mean, I thought I did for a second, but I don't. The woman I was thinking of isn't in Liverpool now.'

'Are you sure, sir.'

'Yeah, yeah. I've got no idea who could have done this. Somebody who doesn't like me, obviously.'

Billy made his way into the house and was greeted first by his mother. He made the usual noises and went into the kitchen where his father was sitting with a cup of tea in front him. Billy sat down opposite him.

'I'm really sorry about this, Dad, I never - '

Jack raised his hand. 'For once, Billy, this is not entirely your fault. You weren't to know you were gettin' involved with the daughter of Jimmy Roberts. He's bad news. There's no good reason why the daughter should be any different.' Jack raised his head and looked Billy in the eye. 'I know you never raped the girl, Billy, without asking you. But tell me one thing and I'll never raise the subject again. Did you lay one finger on her that she didn't invite?'

'I didn't breath on her, Dad, without her wanting me to.'

235

'That's all I need to hear. What did you tell the copper outside?'

'I never even told him what time it was, Dad.'

'Good. Let's keep it that way.' Jack took a sip of his tea before he carried on. 'This is what we're going to do. I'm going to write that bastard Jimmy Roberts a letter. I'm going to say that so far nobody has given either his or his mad daughter's name to the police. I'm going to tell him that this madness stops now. If he stays away and his daughter leaves you alone, then that will be the end of it. If, however, I see either of their miserable faces again within one hundred yards of my front door, I'll ring the police and press charges. They'll be done for criminal assault, criminal damage, breech of the peace, slander, libel, tresspassing and anything else I can think of. I'll also tell him I'll dedicate my life to making his as miserable as I can.'

'Thanks, Dad,' Billy said, relieved.

'As for you, Billy-me-lad. If I hear you've so much as looked in that girl's direction, your feet won't touch the ground. You'll wish you'd never been born.'

Billy put his hand on his father's shoulder. 'You're a good'n, Dad,' he said quietly.

'Aye,' his father answered, 'and a bloody daft one, too.'

Billy made his way to the door and looked back towards Jack. 'Dad?'

'Yeah?'

'Before you right that letter,' Billy asked,

putting his jacket on and keeping his face straight, 'would it be all right if I saw her for just one last kiss?'

Jack jumped from his seat and chased after him. 'You cheeky little bleeder!' he screamed.

Billy was on his on his toes and down the path, but as he looked over his shoulder he saw his father at the front door laughing.

Billy indulged himself in the rare extravagance of a taxi in order to meet Lola on time. They had arranged to meet at seven and it he was just five minutes early when the black cab pulled up outside the Hope Street entrance of the Philharmonic pub.

Dressed in his black barrathea suit, black suede shoes, white silk shirt and blue polka-dot tie, a few female heads turned in his direction as he moved to a table in the corner. He had barely sat down, though, when Lola made a grand entrance of her own.

She wore a burgandy-coloured dress with a full skirt and red high-heels. The dress was cut away at the shoulder to reveal an ample cleavage and was gathered tight at the waist to excentuate the swing of her hips. Around her neck was a black silk scarf over which her raven-black hair cascaded.

She asked for a sherry and a minute later Billy brought the drink back to the table.

'I'm looking forward to hearing you sing tonight,' Billy said, 'especially as I'll shortly have a vested interest in your performances.'

'You've been to the bank?' she asked, doing little to conceal her anticipation.

'I have,' Billy answered with a smile. 'The money's in my pocket.'

She leaned forward and kissed him on the cheek. 'I'm not singing until after nine o'clock,' she said next, 'but I'll have to get going in a minute.'

'What for?' Billy asked, his disappointment obvious.

'Us profesionals don't just get up on the stage and sing, you know, Billy. We have to rehearse. I've got to go over the numbers I'm doing tonight with the boys in the band. Why don't you have a few drinks around town and come up to the club for nine?'

'Okay,' Billy replied. What she was saying made sense. 'I'm sure I can find a couple of old mates to spend an hour or two with. I know a few lads who drink in the Vines at the end of London Road. I'll take a stroll down there.'

Lola looked at him. 'Mmm. If your going to get involved with a few drinking buddies, mightn't it be an idea to give me the money now?'

Billy laughed. 'You're an eager beaver! I've walked around the streets of the Bronx in New York and never been turned over. But I suppose you're right. I might as well give you the money now as later.'

He glanced aropund the bar to make sure they were not being watched and then passed Lola the crisp banknotes. She immediately put the cash into her handbag and leaned forward to kiss Billy hard on the lips.

'You won't regret this,' she whispered into his ear. Within a moment she was up and gone and Billy sat back with a deep feeling of satisfaction in the pit of his stomach.

When Billy went to the Vines, there was nobody there he knew and he thought his mates were probably away on a trip. He wandered down to the American Bar and then the Crown, over the road from Lime Street Station. After a boaring hour-and-a-half, he took a slow walk back up towards the Havana Club, stopping for a glass on the way.

At five-to-nine, he presented himself at the entrance to the club. 'I'm here to see Lola,' he said to the girl sat at the reception desk.

'Aren't they all,' she replied dryly.

'I'm here to see her personally,' Billy went on. 'We're good friends. She's expecting me.'

The girl looked up with a sympathetic smile. 'Well, if she's here, I haven't seen her.'

Billy frowned. 'What do you mean? She's working here tonight.'

'No, she's not. She sometimes comes in for a drink when she's not appearing, but she hasn't been here tonight.'

'Not appearing here?' The muscles of Billy's stomach tightened. 'You mean she's not booked here tonight?'

'No,' she said, 'she never is. Sometimes of a weekend she'll get up and give a song or two with the boys. But that's all.'

At that moment, Mitch Morris came down the stairs. Billy stepped across the foyer to talk to him.

'Excuse me,' Billy said. 'Mr Morris?'

'Yes?'

'I'm looking for Lola. Has she been here tonight?'

The man shook his head. 'I haven't seen her since last Saturday.'

Billy nodded. 'I was only with her a couple of hours ago.'

'Can't help you, son, but she's probably with Maurice.'

'Maurice?'

'Maurice Streslov. A Blackpool lad. That's who she's usually with.'

'You mean her promoter?' Billy asked, trying vainly to put the pieces together.

Mitch laughed. 'Her promoter? Has she spun that yarn on you as well? No, Maurice is her fancy fella.' Mitch looked at Billy's crestfallen face and realised what he was he was confronted with. 'Have you given her some money?'

Billy did not answer, which for Mitch was answer enough. 'I don't know how she finds you fellas, though on reflection maybe I do.' He looked at Billy with as much sympathy as he could muster. 'I'm afraid you and your money have been forever parted, son. Lola is a good singer, but she's a world class con-artist. You've been done. I don't know her very well, but my guess is you won't see her again.'

Billy felt ill. He knew it was hopeless, but he left the club and ran up Hardman Street into Hope Street, not stopping until he arrived outside number thirty-three. The house was in darkness, but Billy still rang the bell and knocked on the door. Sitting on the step, he put his head in his hands. He found it hard to believe. Me, he thought, Billy Walsh, ripped off by a woman. Thank God I haven't told anyone about the fortune I was going to make in showbusiness.

49

Wednesday
7pm

The following night, Billy was in the Knotty Ash Hotel with Vic.

'Ready for another?' Vic asked. 'You look like you need it.'

'Yeah, but let's go to town. I've got to be sure of something.'

Half-an-hour later, they were sat outside Lola's house, where they stayed for twenty minutes before Billy was satisfied there was nobody at home. During that time, he confided in Vic about how stupid he had been.

'Let's go to the Philharmonic. I'd like to ask around about Lola.'

'You're going to have to put this down to experience, Billy, although I don't know how much experience you need before you'll learn anything.'

Billy remembered the barman from the night before and after ordering two pints, asked him if he remembered him being there with a woman in a burgandy dress.

'Can't say as I remember you, pal, but I certainly remember the lady. Wow!'

'Do you know her?'

'Unfortunately, no,' he said with a smile. 'But

it's funny you should ask about her. Some fella was in an hour ago doing the same. Poured his heart out to me, he did. Said she'd conned him out of five hundred pounds. She told him she was going to be a big star in London, was going to make a hit record in the next few weeks, but needed someone to back her with a few serious shillings. He hasn't seen her since he gave her the money. Going mad he was.'

It all sounded painfully familiar to Billy. They sat down at the same table he had been at with Lola the night before. He was finding it difficult to take in.

They finished their drinks and left the pub. As they climbed back into the car parked outside, Billy suddenly had a thought.

'She made a mistake,' he said quietly, a smile breaking over his face.

'What?' Vic asked, turning the ignition.

'She made a bloody mistake! The first time I saw her I was with Carol. She gave me her telephone number on a book of matches. They were from the Scafell Hotel in Lord Nelson Street. That's where she'll be. That will be one of her fancy fella's hotels.'

'She wouldn't be that careless, Billy,' Vic said sceptically.

'She wasn't careless. At that time, she didn't know she'd see me again.'

'Still seems a bit of a long shot,' Vic insisted.

'I don't think so. This fella she told me was her promoter, Maurice Sreslov, the one who turns

243

out to be her boyfriend, she said he had a couple of hotels in Liverpool. I'll bet a pound to a penny that's one of them. Let's go and have a look.'

Five minutes later, Vic pulled up outside the Scafell Hotel.

'How are you going to handle this, Billy?'

Billy thought for a moment. 'She doesn't know you, so if she's there and sees you, it doesn't matter.'

'Okay,' Vic said. 'What do you want me do?'

Two minutes later, Vic was at the hotel's small reception desk.

'Can I help you?' the young, blonde receptionist asked.

'I don't know,' Vic answered. 'I have a message for a Miss Lola Lovelady. I've not been able to catch her at home, but I'm told she can sometimes be located her.'

The young woman smiled. 'Yes, she can,' she said. 'And in your in luck. She's in the residents' lounge right now with the propritor, Mr Strevlos. I'll fetch her you.'

Vic's heart missed a beat. 'No need,' he said. 'Don't disturb her. I have something for her in the car. I'll go and get it and you can pass it on to her.'

'Fine,' the girl said.

Vic was back at the car in a few seconds and gave Billy the news.

'Right,' he said quickly. 'You wait here.' With that, he got out of the car and strode over to the hotel.

'What are you going to do, Bill?' Vic shouted

after him, but he did not answer. 'Well, be bloody careful then,' Vic added.

Billy walked straight past the receptionist and into the resident's lounge. There he saw Lola sitting at the bar with a man he assumed to be Maurice Streslov. He walked over to her and stood between the pair. Lola looked up and her jaw dropped when she looked up at Billy. She was unable to speak.

'Hello, Lola,' Billy said, smiling. 'Lost your tongue?'

'Billy,' she said, the word sticking in her throat. 'What a . . . pleasant surprise.'

'Oh, I'll bet it is, but I really can't stop. If you could just let me have the package you've been holding for me, I'll be on my way.'

'Package?' Lola asked. 'What package?'

Billy sighed. 'There's two ways we can do this, Lola. You can let me have what's mine or I can make an awful lot of fuss. Personally, I'll enjoy both.'

Maurice leaned forward. 'Who the hell are you, friend?' he asked.

Billy turned on him. 'Don't call me friend, buster. You keep out of this and be better for it.' He turned again to Lola. 'Well, which way are we doing this?'

Without speaking, Lola picked up her handbag from the floor and fumbled through its contents. Eventually, she pulled out Billy's money.

He took it from her and put it straight into his pocket. 'Is it all there?'

Lola would not look at him as she answered. 'Er, no, not quite,' she stuttered. 'It's about thirty pounds light. I had to - '

Billy raised a hand. 'I can live with that. Let's call it a payment for the very special services you provided me with on Monday.'

Maurice stood up and confronted Billy. 'Now, listen here, I'm not —'

Billy shoved him hard in the chest and Maurice stumbled back onto his stool. 'No, mate, you listen! It's not my business that you're happy to be seen with this thieving whore.' Billy looked back at Lola, whose eyes were filling with tears. 'But this money is my business. I'll see you around, Lola. Good luck with your singing.'

He then turned and walked quickly from the lounge and rejoined Vic in the car. From the smile on Billy's face, Vic knew it had gone well.

'Got your money?' he asked him.

'All but thirty quid,' Billy answered. 'But I got value for money for that, didn't I?'

Both men laughed and Vic started the car. 'Where to now?' Vic asked.

'Let's get the car parked up and have a good night out, Vic. I owe you one.'

'That's an understatement,' Vic said, smiling broadly, 'but I'm right behind you, so the sooner we get home the better.'

50

One week later

The Sylvania was tied up at the Princes landing stage ready to set sail for New York. Billy was back in harness in the engine room and had remade his acquaintence with the chief engineer, Mr MacDonald. They knew each other well and the man was glad to see Billy back at work.

With a head of steam up and all the checks and inspections completed, the great liner was ready to leave port when the passengers were on board and the tide was right. Billy was finished for a few hours and decided to go for a cup of tea. Standing at the top of the crew's companion way, he watched the passengers come on board. He had been there only a few minutes when he noticed a tall, slim and very elegant woman in a full-length leather suit. The skirt finished just above the knee and she showed a very shapely leg. Her open-neck blouse comcealed a small, pert bust. Around her neck she wore a double string of pearls.

She was struggling with two heavy suitcases, and Billy was quick to assume this could only mean she was travelling alone. The other porters were busily preoccupied and had been unable to assist Mrs Gloria Van Holden. Billy stepped forward to oblige.

'Please,' Billy offered, 'allow me to help you.'

'Why, thank you, young man,' she purred in a sharp, Manhattan accent. 'That sure was a steep climb up there. I'm in cabin twenty-seven.'

Billy took the bags from her and made his way to the cabin. 'Are you on your own?' Billy asked.

'Yes.' She answered. 'I lost my husband three years ago. During the war he was in US Air Force, based here at Burtonwood. That's where I've been.'

They arrived at Cabin twenty-seven and Billy opened the door. Placing the bags inside, he turned to leave.

'Enjoy you're trip home,' he said and made to leave.

'What's your name?' she asked him.

'Billy, ma'am,' he answered.

'Are you working now?'

'Not until eight o'clock.'

The woman smiled and raised a hand to Billy's cheek. 'Then stay a while, Billy. I'm in need of some company.'

Billy closed the door and stepped towards her. Old habits die hard, Billy thought to himself. This could turn out to be a one way trip.